HELL SENT

ALSO BY NINA K. WESTRA

Demons of Ardani

Demon Bound

Hell Sent

Elves of Ardani

Night Elves of Ardani

Rogue Elves of Ardani

Sun Elves of Ardani

Dark Elves of Ardani

Hell Sent

Demons of Ardani
Book 1.5

Nina K. Westra

CONTENTS

ONE

Azreth was hungry. But that was nothing new. To be a demon was to hunger.

So when a presence prodded at the edges of his senses, he picked up an obsidian dagger and crept to the entrance of his tiny shelter—a narrow gap in the earth that he'd disguised with black scrub branches.

He squinted at the barren fields and cracked earth of the fourth plane of hell. Mountains like jagged teeth rose up in the distance, their stark faces unwelcoming and impassable, and the Great Canyon cut the landscape in half. The ever-present winds blew red sand into his eyes, and he blinked rapidly. He saw nothing. Heard nothing.

Demons were like the hells in many ways. They were both eternal and unchanging. Both violent and cruel. Both lonesome and empty.

Or perhaps that last one was just Azreth.

He crawled silently out of the cave, keeping low to the ground. Briefly, he considered dispelling his arm and summoning a magical shield around himself instead. It had been too long since he'd fed, and he didn't want to expend the energy for both.

He glanced down at his right arm and flexed the fingers of the facsimile, their unnatural transparent magenta contrasting with the natural deep blue skin of his left hand. The magic that replaced his missing limb was a small but constant drain on his energy. It was a luxury he couldn't necessarily afford, but he couldn't bring himself to go without it.

The last time he'd fed had been almost two weeks ago, when a fellow outcast had ambushed him while he hunted a velraven. Azreth had gotten lucky. He'd won the fight despite bad odds. His dubious reward was a solitary meal of the other demon's fear and pain as he bled out.

Hunger, as always, gnawed at him.

"Azreth," called a low, feminine voice.

He relaxed a fraction. He recognized the voice—but that didn't mean it was a friend. There were no friends among the kin, only temporary alliances.

He couldn't see her yet, so he stayed low. "Nariel," he replied.

She stepped out from behind a gnarled, petrified tree to his left. Her hands were at her sides, and she carried no weapons. Nariel was tall and strong, with long legs and a full chest shielded by obsidian armor, and her skin was a particular shade of deep violet that he admired more than he liked to admit.

Azreth frowned. He would have to find another place to shelter after this. Now that she knew to look for him here, it was not safe.

She looked him up and down, assessing his health. If he seemed weak, she might decide to try to overpower him. In the end, she seemed to decide he looked strong enough. "I must feed," she said flatly, her frown unchanging. "Shall we come together?"

He nodded. They fed from each other often. It was mutually beneficial, for now.

He put his dagger on the ground. Nariel came closer, unlatching her breastplate and sarong and letting them drop to the ground, leaving her bare. Azreth felt an annoying twinge in his loins.

He had heard that sex was different for mortals. They actually enjoyed it. Nariel enjoyed it too, he thought, but not like mortals did. It was always dangerous to be so close to another demon. They were never safe. They felt no love for each other.

His sexual desire was a vulnerability. It was a commodity to be traded or stolen. And he disliked the way his arousal could come without his permission. He would have disposed of it entirely if he could, but then he would have nothing to offer her.

He let out a slow breath. There was no point being annoyed or wishing things were something other than what they were. It was unproductive. He untied his sarong and let it slip off his hips, leaving him clad only in his tall, armored boots.

Nariel waited a few steps from him, her arms crossed beneath her breasts. Her eyes tracked over his body, flicking across his angled horns and his hands. She wasn't admiring him—she was checking for hidden weapons or spells, and for weaknesses.

She was physically bigger than he was, but he knew his magic was stronger. They would be an even match in a fight, which was why they got along. But it was generally agreed upon among demonkind that the party being penetrated was at a natural disadvantage during intercourse. She would not agree to be penetrated *and* pinned on her back. So, he reluctantly sank to the ground and lay on his back, as he always did.

Nariel gracefully dropped to her knees atop him, straddling his hips. Her bright eyes were on his as she wrapped a hand around his stiffening cock. The muscles in his thighs tensed, and he hoped she would think it was only from arousal and not discomfort.

"Still healthy, I see," she said with a smirk. "For a cripple."

He glared at her and raised his hand to the triangle between her legs, weaving a spell. "I will prepare you?" he murmured.

She nodded once. "And I you?"

"Yes."

With perfunctory permission obtained, they pressed magic into each other. Her spell sank into him more aggressively than he'd expected. His cock went rigid and tightened painfully, and he bucked against her hand, needing to be inside something. He pushed his own spell into her, commanding her body to open for him. She clenched her jaw to hide her reaction, but he could feel it. It wafted over him like sweet perfume. Lifting him with her hand, she aligned him with her entrance and then sank onto him with a sigh.

They entered a familiar rhythm as her hands braced against his chest—a cycle of both physical pleasure and feeding from each other's emotional energy. They did not speak, and they did not touch each other more than necessary. The wrong sort of touch could easily be mistaken for an attack. He felt his strength building and draining at once. As her pleasure built, so did his power.

He hated this—the sense of losing control. The need to thrust and climax and feed threatened to overcome him, and he feared he couldn't stop even if he wanted to. He was torn between resisting it and submitting to it.

In a moment of weakness, he let himself reach up and hold one of Nariel's breasts. She was soft and supple, her warm flesh giving in his grasp. Privately, he thought there was something wonderful about touching soft things. Most things in the hells were hard or rough or sharp.

Instead of rebuking him, Nariel smirked. She clenched around his cock, her thighs squeezing him. Her body undulated as she worked to wring pleasure from him.

His eyes fluttered closed and his hands clenched on her thigh and her breast as he reached climax. He thrust to her deepest point, anchoring himself to her, basking in her body. Through the haze of the orgasm, he felt her leaning closer.

And then pain ripped through him.

He roared, snapping back to reality in an instant. Her black hair shrouded his face, obstructing his vision, but he felt her sharp teeth buried in his neck, ripping violently. She clenched her jaw, cutting through flesh, and he felt his own hot blood pouring over his skin.

He tried to push her away, but she grabbed his wrists and slammed them to the ground. Her legs were tangled in his, holding him down. Her teeth were cutting through him inch by inch.

He dispelled his false arm from beneath her grasp, and she pitched forward, surprised. In its place, he summoned another, this time sharpening its fingers to daggerlike points, and stabbed it toward her.

Nariel flinched, black blood streaming from her cheek and dripping from her teeth. There was a shallow cut from her ear to her nose. Azreth struck again, fighting through fiery agony to sling a flurry of magical knives at her.

As she ducked and swatted at the knives, Azreth scrambled backward, clutching his throat. He was already too late. His neck was open from ear to ear, and he could see—*hear*—blood spurting from an open artery. He tried to speak, and nothing came out of his mouth except blood.

His fingers slipped in the streaming blood as he forced

magic into the wound. As he focused on the healing spell, he lost control of the summoned knives attacking Nariel, and they dissolved, but the bleeding started to slow. The edges of the tear began to seal over, but then Nariel dove for him again.

He leapt backward, but her fist caught his chin, knocking him sideways. Her hands clamped around his damaged throat, and she wrestled him to the ground.

She said nothing. There was no explanation, no apology, not even any gloating. Just cruelty, fear, and hunger.

He waved a hand, magic crackling at his fingers but not quite coalescing into a spell before she hit his hand away. His vision pulsed black as she choked him, and he curled his fingers into a fist, forcing magic to bend to his will as he fought to stay conscious. Nariel drew back her fist, about to deal what would undoubtedly be a killing blow. Azreth thrust his spell forward.

A magenta blade speared through one side of her head and out the other.

She went still, her eyes suddenly empty and unfocused. Her fingers twitched on him, their hold still tight, as if they'd been frozen in death.

Azreth struggled out from beneath her and shoved her aside, gasping for breath. He let the blade dissolve as he refocused his magic on healing his throat. Slowly, his flesh began knitting back together. Coughing, he spat out a dark clot of blood and ran his fingers gingerly over the ragged gash. It was still bleeding, but it would stop soon.

Nariel's eyes had gone cold and dark, their glow almost extinguished. Azreth considered her, scowling. He could have left her where she lay, to serve as a warning to others. But the body would attract scavengers, and more importantly, it would smell.

Snarling, he picked her up. As he stood, his knees almost

gave out from under him. All the energy he'd gained from her had immediately been used to fight her, and now he was even more drained than before.

His feet slid in loose sand as he trudged down the hillside toward the river bank behind his shelter. Nariel drooped lifelessly in his arms, her head bouncing against his chest.

He had no right to be angry. This was his own fault. She'd sensed him lowering his guard, and she'd taken advantage, as anyone would have. He'd given in to the temptation to trust her, and he'd made a target of himself. It was like dangling a baby nyx in front of a velraven.

He dropped her beside the river of flame, then knelt next to her, panting from exertion. The river oozed, waves of heat rising from its molten surface.

If he thought about it, he supposed that he had liked her —as much as he could like anyone. Her presence had been a threat, but it had also been a break in the emptiness of the wasteland and the vast solitude that was his life. He wasn't happy she was dead.

He pushed her over the edge of the bank, and the liquid fire slowly carried her away. Resisting the urge to stare after her, he waded into the fire to wash away the blood sticking to his skin.

For a long time, he sat on the river bank, occasionally clearing his throat and spitting up more blood. He watched the crimson sky churn with storms, clouds racing towards the horizon.

Sitting out in the open like this was another luxury he hadn't earned. Anyone could come upon him and kill him before he could defend himself. But he did not look up to make sure no flying creatures were descending on him. He didn't glance over his shoulder to make sure there was no one coming up behind him, even though he was in a vulnerable position at the bottom of a hill. In fact, he closed his eyes, shutting out the world. The bubbling of the river obstructed his hearing. If anything else came upon him, he wouldn't know until it was too late, and he would die.

Survival was tiresome.

And yet, when he heard a sound to his left, he spun, ready to fight for his life again.

The sound was an odd hissing, like steam jetting from a volcanic vent. Upriver, a shimmer had appeared in midair. Before his eyes, it grew, the sound increasing to a harsh whine.

The shimmer turned into a window to somewhere else. Wind and magic poured through it, hitting Azreth in bursts. Through the window, two male faces appeared, staring back at him. They were close together, almost fighting over space to peer through the small opening.

They were mortals. Azreth stared at them in disbelief.

The taller of the two lifted his chin, glaring out at Azreth imperiously. "You. Come here." He said it like an order. Awfully presumptuous, considering Azreth could probably crush him with one hand. The man thought he was safe behind whatever magic he'd used to open the window.

He was not the first demon to be summoned by a greedy mortal. Naturally small and fragile, mortals lusted for power the way demons hungered for lust. Their mages only reached across the planes into the hells when they wished to enslave a demon.

That was what he'd heard. But he had never been so lucky as to see it happen. This was the sort of opportunity that came only once in a lifetime.

He walked closer. The mortals shifted, practically vibrating with excitement and fear. Avarice shone in their eyes as he stopped in front of the window.

"Good," the taller one said, approving of his obedience.

The shorter man wore a plain black robe and was shaved

bald. But the taller one wore elaborate clothing with metal and fur details and many different colors of thread. His long hair was perfectly cleaned and combed, smoothed with oils or tonics. Azreth wondered if he was someone of high status, or if all mortals had the time and means for such frivolous things. Maybe they were all this arrogant, too.

Both of them were pale and small. Frail. Breakable.

"I have an offer to make you, demon," the taller man said. "Serve me here in the mortal realm, and I will ensure you never go hungry. Would you like that? To have unfettered access to an entire plane of mortals? Come to me, and you can kill and feed to your black heart's content."

They thought they were clever. And they thought he was an imbecile.

They were right about one thing: he wanted them. How could anyone resist the opportunity to go to a plane where emotion ran free and wild, waiting to be devoured? It was a thing demons dreamed of.

The only problem was that mortals were clever about their summonings. There would be a cage waiting on the other side of the portal. That was how mortals worked. They summoned demons to trap them and force them into service —until the demon found a way to escape their servitude, at least.

Azreth looked around at the stark landscape—his awful home. He looked downstream, where Nariel had sunk beneath the flames of the river. He thought about the times he'd starved for weeks, the surprise attacks by other demons in the night, having to lie on his back and grit his teeth through feedings, and all the betrayals from kin he'd wished he could trust.

What was hell if not one enormous cage?

Perhaps even a life in a mortal's cage would be better than a life in the hells. Or at least, it couldn't be worse.

After all, demons were ageless and infinite. He could wait a long, long time for his freedom.

The taller mortal glanced over at the shorter one. "Does it understand? Perhaps they don't know our language."

Azreth stepped forward. The mortals started and backed away as he climbed into the window.

Two

The whistling of air and magic being squeezed through too little space increased as he entered the portal, and wind rushed in his ears. Somehow, even as he climbed inside, the mortals on the other side didn't get any closer. As he passed through the entrance, the portal expanded, turning into a long corridor in front of him. The walls were both featureless white and filled with flashes of color, a contradiction he couldn't explain, and he could not be sure whether they were collapsing in on him or unfolding to become larger. He sensed infinity expanding on every side of him, as if he were standing at the edge of a thousand cliffs, falling past a million skies. He pushed onward, even though the ground had disappeared beneath him and he couldn't feel his legs.

Abruptly, the infinite space shrank again, and he burst through the window, face down onto a cold, stone floor. The portal snapped shut behind him.

After the howling of the tunnel between planes, the quiet of this place was deafening. Soft footsteps rushed around. Someone was chanting.

"Hurry up," hissed a familiar voice. The arrogant mortal.

As Azreth looked up to take in his new surroundings, magic came to life around him. The chanting of the shorter mortal had activated a spell. Walls of magic rose up around him, enclosing him in a small cell: the cage he'd been expecting.

He was inside a dark, cavernous room made of stone. Perhaps it was underground, for there were no windows. It was empty except for the two mortals and himself, as if it existed only to hold him. He wrinkled his nose. Inhaling the air here was like eating meat that had gone cold—slimy and stale and unpleasant. He wondered if all of the mortal plane had this scent, or if it was just this room.

His magical cage was a transparent barrier of solid magic, not unlike the spell he used for his false arm—which was gone. He glanced down at his shoulder. He'd lost concentration on the spell when he'd traveled through the portal, and he didn't have the magic to expend on it now, anyway.

It didn't matter. He wouldn't need to fight any of his own kind here. He could face humans just as easily with one arm as he could with two. With mortals, it was their minds that were dangerous, not their bodies.

The taller mortal stepped closer to the barrier. "I am Lord Nirlan Han-gal. I am your master."

Azreth drove his fist into the barrier. The mortals flinched.

It felt like punching air, but there was a sharp *bang* as the magic stopped him from passing through. He tried several more times for good measure, but it had no effect on the barrier. He hadn't thought it would work, but it would have been foolish not to try, wouldn't it?

Lord Nirlan chuckled, watching with awe. "What a brute. Look at him go." He leaned closer. "Can you understand me, or not?"

Azreth bent low to examine the seam where the barrier

connected to the floor. He could sense the magic continuing through the ground beneath him. He would not be able to dig under it.

"I think he can," Lord Nirlan said, either to himself or to the other man. Then, after a pause, "It's missing an arm. Of all the demons in every hell, this is the one you brought me?"

The robed mortal finally spoke. His voice was low and serious. "The spell is not like an arrow I can easily shoot where I wish. It is not so simple to dictate what comes through it."

"Of course. Wonderful."

Azreth raised his hand, connecting to the web of magic that, to his relief, coated this world just like his own. He plucked at the strings of the spell holding together the barrier. It was strong—more complex than any magic he understood. He had no hope of unraveling it.

Instead, he curled his fingers into a fist, summoning a blade of magic. The mortals' eyes widened, and the lord took half a step back.

Azreth jammed the blade into the barrier. Or, he tried to. The blade dissolved into nothing when it touched the barrier.

The mortal lord relaxed. "You're quite violent, aren't you?"

Azreth exhaled heavily, finally looking down at the man.

He would wait. His keepers would slip up eventually. And then he would destroy them.

<hr>

AZRETH HAD SEEN MORTALS BEFORE, but only a handful of times. They were kept as feeding slaves whenever they were captured in the hells. On a few occasions, he had crossed paths with one of them trailing another demon. It had made him burn with envy. He was fairly confident he could milk a single human for decades without killing them, if he was careful—

and if he could tolerate the ugliness of the slaves. All of them had a wide-eyed, hollow look to them, like their minds were already dead and their bodies had gone on without them. He was disgusted by how sad and small and helpless they were.

He'd never fed from a mortal, but he knew they were easily frightened and easily controlled. He also knew that feeding from them was nothing like feeding from another demon. Nariel had fed from mortals before. When he'd asked her about it, she'd looked wistful and said it was like comparing freshly killed meat to dry, moldering bones.

That was what he'd heard, at least. That was what he imagined as he watched the human lord and his mage coming in and out of his chamber over the next few days. He envisioned killing them in various ways, and he thought about how lovely their agony would taste.

The bald mage, whom the lord called Eunaios, spent many hours painting enchanting runes all over the stones of the walls and floor. Now that he'd summoned and trapped Azreth, he was beginning work on a new spell.

Eunaios would work alone, in silence, for hours at a time without glancing up at him, but whenever he did, he looked nervous. Azreth stared straight back at him, hoping his fear—which was difficult to feel through the barrier—would intensify. It did, but only enough to whet his appetite.

After a long session of painting on the floor, Eunaios stood up, wincing as his joints cracked. Rubbing his lower back, the man looked over at him. Azreth was surprised when the mage actually came closer.

He stopped right beside the cage, squinting at him with a challenge in his eyes. "You always watch me. Why? Do you think you can intimidate me?" Eunaios said, his voice muffled by the barrier.

Azreth didn't know what to say to that, so he said nothing.

Eunaios backed away, and Azreth thought that was the end of the interaction, but he was only fetching something that hung from a hook on the wall. A metal baton.

"Do you know what this is?" the mage asked, brandishing it.

Azreth just looked at him.

Eunaios pointed the baton toward the cage. Azreth had time to register the runes carved into it and the gathering of light at its tip just before lightning shot from it. It passed straight through the barrier and struck him like an iron sword. His vision went white as pain jolted through him. The next thing he knew, he was crumpled on the floor. Azreth panted, trembling.

"Do you even know what power I have?" Eunaios said, sounding far away. "I alone brought you here. Not Nirlan. It was I who summoned you here, and I who will bind you. Look at me again, demon."

Slowly, he looked up at Eunaios. The baton exploded into crackling lightning again. Azreth tried to summon a shield to block the attack, but magic only sparked uselessly at his fingertips. He'd not fed, so he still had no power.

The lightning cut through him, burning him from the inside out. He tried to crawl backwards, but he hit the back of his cage.

Finally, the attack stopped.

"And now?" the mage said, his voice shaking ever so slightly. "Look at me again. Do you dare?"

Azreth began to look up, then stopped himself. He kept his eyes on the ground, bracing himself for another attack.

Eunaios huffed, straightening. When he turned away, Azreth watched him return the baton to its hook on the wall before he left.

The days seemed to get longer. There was no sun nor moons visible from his cell to track the time, so he could only judge its passing based on the comings and goings of his captors. They did not seem to plan on letting him out of the cage any time soon.

Several times a day at least, he tested the barrier again. It always held, and he became more tired each time he tried it. He could feel himself growing more feeble by the hour.

Was this really better than the hells?

Yes, of course it was. Or it would be, if he was patient.

He'd assumed that the humans had brought him here to use him—not just to let him die here. Was it possible that they didn't understand how the kin lived? Perhaps they didn't know that he'd die if he was left down here without feeding for long enough.

The next time Eunaios came to paint his runes, Azreth reluctantly spoke to him.

"I require sustenance," he said, disliking that he had to beg. But if they truly meant to bind him, this was only the beginning of many indignities he would suffer at their hands before he found a way to escape them.

Eunaios looked up sharply, then narrowed his eyes. "So you do speak, after all."

"Yes."

Eunaios studied him. "You'll have your sustenance soon enough."

"How soon?"

"Why? Are you desperate?"

Azreth said nothing. He wished the man would come closer. Perhaps he'd be careless and let one of his billowy sleeves graze through the barrier wall. Azreth would pull him through, and he'd be dead before he could even scream.

"Our *lord*," Eunaios began, putting sarcastic emphasis on the title, "is the one you must ask." He waited, as if expecting Azreth to react. When he didn't, he added, "I'll inform him."

Azreth was left alone for several days more.

The silence, the emptiness of the place, the hunger and helplessness, wore him down. Somewhere in the distance, he could sometimes hear small scurrying animals running through the cracks in the walls. He found himself hanging on every sound, desperate for any stimulus that would break up the time. He began to hear phantom footsteps in the hallway every now and then. He would sit up, staring at the dark doorway for long minutes, only to eventually realize there was no one coming. He grew strangely nervous, jumping at the creaking of stone or drips of moisture through wet rock.

He'd been beaten and tortured and nearly killed many times before. But he'd never been trapped like this, alone with no magic, no way to fight, no control, no paths forward. It was a kind of slow torture. It made his limbs itch, like there were insects crawling under his skin. Waiting, and waiting, and waiting.

Until finally, the woman came.

THREE

Azreth sensed her coming before she stepped through the door. He was so starved that even through the barrier, he could sense the spark of her emotions. Her fear.

Lord Nirlan, smiling a little, dragged her through the doorway, and her eyes focused on Azreth just as intently as his did on her.

Was she for him?

This was the third mortal he'd met up close, but the first female. She was human, like the others, but she looked different from the males. Slightly smaller and finer-boned. Her skin wasn't quite as pale as Nirlan's. Instead, it was a faintly earthen color, and her hair was as shiny black as his own. Her eyes were dark and somehow seemed more watchful than the others'.

Nirlan shoved the woman closer, and she fell to her knees in front of Azreth. She looked up at him with her eyes wide, her lips slightly parted. Fear spilled from her, and it was like wine pouring down his throat.

Salivating, he leaned closer to the barrier. He'd heard that mortal blood was sweet and bright red, like the juice of some rare fruit. The woman's skin was thin, and he could see the flutter of her panicked heartbeat in her delicate throat, her veins plump and ripe.

He forced himself to pull back a little. He couldn't bite her. She might die. He didn't know how long it would be before they gave him another mortal to feed from. He couldn't waste this one.

"Nirlan, please don't do this," he heard the woman say, her voice small and distant through the barrier.

Nirlan was smiling faintly. His hand was on the back of her neck, which might have passed for a loving caress if not for the way her skin was turning white where his fingers dug into her. "Don't do what?"

"Feed me to it." There was a slight crack in her voice. Though she spoke to Nirlan, she was still staring at Azreth, her eyes shining.

"What makes you think I'd feed my own wife to a demon?"

Azreth's gaze flicked up to Nirlan's in faint surprise. A wife was a mating partner. Mortals liked to pair up for life, sharing homes and children together. They were allies, bound by permanent vows. Or so he'd thought.

Nirlan leaned close to his wife's ear, whispering terrible threats. The way he touched her was almost sensual, even as he was describing how Azreth would flay her alive. His hand traveled down her body and then eased between her legs. The woman's eyes darkened, and the scent of her fear changed, now tinged with shame and... hatred.

Impossibly, Azreth's appetite for her blood began to wane, replaced by irritation.

Not that it mattered. He understood now that she was no sacrifice for him. Nirlan was only using Azreth to threaten the woman. And he was using the woman to taunt Azreth. To

Azreth's chagrin, it worked. Having a meal dangled in front of him was infuriating.

———

WHEN AZRETH GREW TOO weak to sit up anymore, he curled up on the bottom of his cage. Eunaios would occasionally look over at him and frown as he worked. Azreth would blink at him slowly.

He would close his eyes, and even though he couldn't quite sleep, time seemed to pass more quickly that way.

He half-dreamed while he half-slept. He would imagine escaping and sucking the humans dry, but then he would rouse himself and realize he was still in his cage.

He dreamed of the dark-eyed woman. In the dream, her face entranced him, like she'd cast a spell that kept him from looking anywhere but her. Her pulse pounded visibly in her throat, teasing him.

He would probably die soon.

He regretted never tasting the freedom he'd imagined he might have here.

But there was no point in regretting things. It was irrational and unproductive.

———

IN A HALF-DREAM, he saw the river he'd tossed Nariel into. He could feel the warmth of the flames. The heat was inviting. He tried to move closer, but his limbs were leaden.

Slowly, he opened his eyes. His cursed cell swam into focus. Before him, there was a figure on the ground. His vision sharpened.

There was a mortal in the cage with him.

When she saw that he'd awakened, she tried to scramble

backwards. Azreth lunged for her. She shouted as he grabbed her and pulled her back. He was only vaguely aware of her skinny limbs kicking and slapping at him as he flipped her onto her back and pinned her by her throat. The bloodlust overpowered everything else.

Terror filled the space between them, washing over him, and he could not get close enough, could not have enough. It spiked his hunger, and suddenly he was ravenous, his body empty and wanting. The back of his throat flexed in anticipation of feeding. His stomach twisted on itself, desperate to be filled. All of his senses were focused on the heat of the body beneath him, the pumping of its blood and the thick, heavy waves of fear flowing from it, pulsing in his ears and clouding his eyes. A river of emotion exploded across his skin, drowning him.

He bent toward the source of the river, pressing his mouth to a fluttering vein. The scent of flesh filled his nose. His teeth itched to sink deep into it, to tear muscle fibers and snap veins and rip strips of fat into broken pieces. He needed to bite and crush and destroy, or he would die, he would go mad—

There was a sound very close to his ear, fighting against the din of his hunger. Screaming.

He couldn't bite her. She would die. He had to stop.

Hunger pounded through him as he pulled away to look down at the mortal. It was the same woman as before. She was crying.

A heavy feeling passed over him like a shadow, numbing his hunger. He paused there, struggling against himself.

And then a sweet, metallic scent reached his nose. He inhaled deeply, looking for the source of the smell. Somehow, the mortal had started bleeding from her fingers.

He lifted her hand, fascinated. The blood was vibrant, beautiful, shining red. It was hard to believe that it had turned out this way through the random chaos of the universe, and that it had not been designed specifically to entice him. He closed his eyes and drew his tongue slowly over her fingers.

It tasted like sunlight. He'd never experienced anything like it.

As he tasted her blood and her warm skin, he was surprised to find himself imagining licking her sex this way. How would her arousal taste? He pictured her writhing in ecstasy beneath him, overwhelmed with pleasure.

She'd never allow that. No mortal would willingly allow a demon to touch them.

"Tell me what you want," she whispered.

Azreth looked down at the woman. Her tears were drying on her cheeks, and her gaze was intense and focused and furious. She had stopped trying to wriggle free of his grasp.

"Make my death quick and painless, and I'll give you whatever you want," she said quietly. An idea seemed to come to her, and her eyes brightened. "I will tell you about Nirlan. You want to kill him, don't you? I'll help you escape. I'll help you kill him."

With his mind still hazy with hunger, he couldn't quite make sense of this. It was the last thing he'd expected her to say.

"Please," she whispered. Azreth's insides twisted a little.

Light exploded through the barrier, and pain juddered through him. He released the woman, rolling backwards as several more blasts hit him. The baton again.

By the time he could see straight again, the woman was outside the barrier. He could hear the mortal lord arguing with her.

Azreth warily sat up, and the lord sneered at him. "Soon you'll be bound to me. Then we can let you out, and you can wreak havoc on the countryside. You'd like that, wouldn't you?" He pointed the baton toward him, and lightning burst forth again. Azreth gasped, crumpling.

Nirlan tossed the baton aside. There was something intentional about the casual way he did it, as if to show them all how little he cared about any of them.

As Azreth watched them go, he fantasized about separating Nirlan's head from his body.

FOUR

Eunaios stayed carefully outside the barrier as he used levitation magic to install chains linked to the floor and ceiling, then held Azreth still in a kneeling position and placed a collar around his neck and a manacle around his wrist. As soon as Azreth felt the mage's magic release him, he heaved at the chains, and was surprised to find that they held fast. They were not iron, but they may as well have been.

He glanced down at the runes glowing on the floor beside him. The chains, and the stone they were anchored in, had been enchanted somehow to prevent them from breaking.

He glared at Eunaios, who was smirking a little, pleased with his work. "What is this for?"

"You're going to be bound," Eunaios said coolly. "As we've told you. You may as well save your strength. You won't escape."

Azreth disliked him almost as much as he disliked the lord.

When Eunaios was sure Azreth was held fast, he disabled the barrier, then came close and began painting runes on Azreth's body. The black ink glided over his skin and hardened, marking him with a spell to be activated later. He finished before long, then left Azreth alone in the room again.

Azreth pulled against the chains with all his strength. The metal dug into his skin. Barbs on the inside of the collar prodded at him until they tore through, making him bleed. The stone flooring shook, but didn't crack, let alone break.

He closed his eyes, gritted his teeth, and tried to shove down the animalistic fear that had started to claw into his mind. The chains restricted his movement, holding him almost motionless on his knees, and they seemed to pull at his soul as well as his body.

He could survive many creative tortures, but he despised feeling powerless, and that was exactly what he was about to be. He would be owned and controlled by this mortal he hated.

The mortal would die eventually. Azreth could wait it out. He would have to.

But perhaps he'd underestimated the suffering that was possible in the mortal world. He had thought he had the strength to tolerate being owned for a while in exchange for transport to this plane. Maybe he'd been wrong.

He'd gone still again by the time he heard people approaching. He heard many pairs of feet—many more than the three mortals he'd met so far.

He was surprised to see a dozen or so people, guided by Nirlan and Eunaios, pour through the door. They gawked at him, making exclamations of shock and awe.

This was it. The binding spell. With a crowd to witness his defeat, apparently.

Nirlan was addressing the small audience as Eunaios began painting runes on the lord's palms: runes that would bind Azreth to him and subject him to his will. Eunaios was right. There was no escaping.

He saw a timid movement out of the corner of his eye.

The woman was here. He hadn't seen her at first, because she was a little away from all the others, as if she didn't quite belong to the group, which struck him as odd. Maybe he'd been wrong about how mortal mating worked, and a wife was really more of a slave than a partner.

Her eyes slid across the room and stopped when they met his. They looked at each other for a long moment. Her face was hard and stiff with repressed emotion. She must have been furious at Azreth for what he'd done to her last time they'd met.

She came closer, her deep, dark eyes never leaving his. As she came near, he was able to pick out her emotions from the jumble of indistinct mortal feelings filling the room. She was indeed angry, but it was an unexpectedly bitter, cool anger, and when he consumed it, it felt like chewing on uncooked bone.

She stopped just beside him, within arm's reach, and looked at him. Unlike the last time he'd seen her, pale powder covered her face, and delicate black ink ringed her eyes and darkened her brows. Her lips were as red as her blood. She looked like death. Like a pale corpse with a bloodied mouth.

His collar was pulling his head up, baring his throat, forcing him into a position of submission in front of her. He was faintly embarrassed by how he'd been with her before, so out of control, like a starving animal. He wondered if she would have stabbed him if the lord had permitted it. She was the only one of his captors who hadn't hit him with that baton yet, but he didn't know if that was because she was less violent than the others, or if the opportunity just hadn't arisen.

She leaned even closer, looking down on him, and he braced himself to be struck.

"I don't know if you can understand me," she whispered.

"And I know you will likely kill me if I release you. But I would rather die now, on my own terms, than by his hand."

He blinked slowly at her. She was fidgeting. He looked down at her feet, and she was vigorously scratching the floor with her slipper. Vigorously, and stealthily.

"All I ask is that if you must take my life, take his, as well." There was a distinct note of desperation in her voice. She said nothing else, just glanced over her shoulder at the others. Her faint anxiety was blooming into true fear.

With her toe, she was scratching at one of the runes Eunaios had drawn on the ground, and the paint was wearing away. She was... erasing it.

Suddenly, the rune flickered and then went dark, its magic extinguished as she destroyed the mark. She looked up at Azreth, eyes wide, then hurriedly backed away.

From across the room, Nirlan finally took notice of his wife. He frowned at both of them, suspicious. "What are you doing?"

Azreth looked down at the broken rune. Cautiously, he tried pulling the chain attached to his wrist. It easily came up from the ground with a snap.

She'd freed him.

She'd freed him?

The room filled with shouts. The mortals ran from him, fighting over the doorway. Eunaios and Nirlan were closest to him, both watching him with growing horror.

Nirlan grabbed Eunaios. "Finish the spell!"

Azreth shot to his feet, fighting the numbness in his legs as he took the manacle in his teeth and wrenched the metal apart. He grabbed the collar and destroyed it next, and suddenly there was nothing holding him back. In two strides, he'd crossed the room and picked up Eunaios by the front of his robe. The man's eyes were wide as Azreth lifted him high, opened his mouth, and sank his teeth into his throat, cutting off his screams.

Blossom-sweet blood sprayed down Azreth's throat. The mage panicked and raged, writhing and twitching. His emotions blazed and spiraled and then quieted with acceptance of his fate. It was just as good as Azreth had imagined. There was nothing that tasted more exquisite than death.

As he threw aside the mage's body, a burst of warmth hit his side. Confused by the sensation, he turned to see a woman with a ball of magical flame in her hand. He realized it had been an attempt to hurt him. So he went to her and ripped out her throat, too, and again he drowned in delicious anguish.

As he dropped her, he was panting with a sort of ragged, hysterical joy, mortal blood covering his mouth and chest. This was everything he'd dreamed of. He had a sudden, wild urge to laugh.

When a set of guards approached, wearing steel armor and wielding steel blades, he simply picked up one and threw him into the wall, crumpling his armor. The next guard stabbed at Azreth with his ridiculous, brittle sword, which merely glanced off Azreth's skin. The mortal blanched. He started to turn and run, but Azreth knocked him to the ground and pressed his palm to the man's chest, crushing him slowly until his body snapped inward with a satisfying crunch.

As panicked shouts moved down the hallway, Azreth stood at ease, his mind hazy with bloodlust and satisfaction. All the other mortals had wisely run.

Except one. He could smell her fear from across the room.

He turned to look at the dark-eyed woman. The wife. She'd pressed her back against the wall, keeping as far away from him as possible. As he looked at her, her knees buckled, and she slid to the floor. She looked at him like he was a monster. He supposed he was.

Curiosity nagged at him. She'd asked him for death twice now. He'd never met someone so eager to die.

As the mortal blood cooled on his skin, he sobered. There could be other mages here. Other traps. Guards who wielded iron instead of steel. The thought chilled him.

He couldn't let himself be trapped here again. He needed to get out.

He turned and moved down the hallway after the others, leaving the woman to her own devices.

He followed the sounds of mortal cries down the dark tunnels. The building was enormous and labyrinthine. Several times, he was confronted by more guards. He quickly ended them.

He found his way up a flight of ancient steps into an equally ancient building made from blocks of dark gray stone. He was above ground now, and windows on the walls gave him glimpses of a black sky dotted with stars.

That alien sky frightened him. He was in a strange world filled with unexpected dangers. He had avoided becoming enslaved to the mortals, but only narrowly. He needed time to rest and consider his options. He needed to get out of this place.

He came to a set of massive doors at the end of a large hall, and he could smell fresh air leaking through them. He burst through the doors, and suddenly he was outside.

Cold, uninviting air blew over his skin. The sky opened up above him, vast and empty and dark. Ahead of him was a sort of courtyard and another massive wall. A prison inside a prison.

It was a castle. Eunaios and Nirlan had summoned him into its dungeon.

Something hard bounced off his back, and he looked down to find an arrow on the ground beside him. Yet more mortals approached him, one wielding a bow, and the other a sword. The swordsman was the biggest mortal he'd yet seen—a man almost his own height—and yet, unfortunately for the mortal, he was still just a man.

The mortal brandished the useless weapon. "Die, beast!"

Azreth took a long breath, wondering at them as they ran toward their own death. He didn't have the patience or desire for the dramatic flair he'd had downstairs. So he simply stabbed one of them in the throat with the point of the arrow, then bashed in the skull of the other with the hilt of his own sword. He took surprisingly little joy in it.

On the outer wall was a closed gate, through which he could see grass and a dirt road and hills in the distance. But as he got closer, a cold, unpleasant sensation settled over him. A bad energy was coming from the gate. Iron.

Clenching his jaw, he turned his attention to the high walls. He was trying to decide how best to scale or break through them when he heard a panicked breath behind him.

He turned, and there was the dark-eyed woman again, blinking at him in surprise. She'd followed him. The lightning baton rested on her hip like a sword.

He crossed the space between them quickly, taking her by the arm before she could draw the baton. She tried to pull free, and he jerked her back toward him. He hadn't thought he was being overly rough, but her entire body was thrown off by the movement, and she cried out, nearly falling over.

Azreth took a breath, considering what to do next.

He had enough magic now to summon his false arm, so he began working the spell. Magic trickled around the stump of his right shoulder, then coalesced into a perfect mirror of his left arm. It was the most complex spell he knew, but he was well practiced at it. It was complete in seconds.

The woman watched the process closely, as if filing away the information for later. Maybe she disapproved of the broken pretending to be whole. Or perhaps she was thinking of ways to use his infirmity against him.

He pointed to the iron bars. "What will unlock this cage?"

The woman's eyes flicked toward the bars, then back to him. Fear cloaked her like a second skin.

He squeezed her arm tighter when she didn't answer. Her body was as soft as bruised fruit, and he could sense the brittleness of the bone beneath the muscle, narrow and oddly flexible under his grasp. It disturbed him.

It occurred to him that he might have been damaging her, and he loosened his grip slightly. "Speak," he said.

"I—I don't know. I've never seen it down. You could lift it. I'm sure you're strong enough."

"I cannot."

Her eyes returned to the gate, flitting across the bars. "On the wall. There's a lever."

Azreth let his gaze leave her for a moment, just long enough to look. She was telling the truth. There was a handle. A mechanism to open the gate from the inside.

He studied the woman. She'd traded her delicate slippers for sturdy boots at some point during the past few minutes, and she wore a cloak and carried a small traveling bag, now. There was a panicked look in her eyes, but it was a different sort of panic from the others, somehow.

She was just watching him. Waiting.

"Raiya!" Nirlan appeared in the doorway, but he skidded to a halt when he saw Azreth. His eyes darted between them, his expression hovering on the cusp of outrage—and Azreth realized the lord still wanted his wife, even though he'd thrown her carelessly into his cell just a few days ago.

Azreth thought of all the ways he'd fantasized about killing Nirlan. He could disembowel him, crush him, behead him. He could take the baton and shoot him with lightning until it ran out of magic.

As Nirlan took a step backward, Azreth almost chased him back inside the castle. Back inside his prison. Back where he'd been trapped, unable to move, unable to feed or weave magic.

Fear pulsed through him, extinguishing the bloodlust. His heart pounded. He needed to escape. He needed to run.

He was afraid. He was weak.

The woman had stopped trying to pull away. She took half a step toward Azreth, putting him between herself and Nirlan. Azreth came to a decision. He picked her up and held her across his chest. She yelped in surprise.

"Be still," he warned her quietly, and a part of him was worried she would fight, and that he'd have to hurt her. He was surprised to realize how much he did not want to do that.

She'd saved him. Even if she'd only done it to hurt the lord, he was grateful.

Fortunately, she went rigid and motionless against his chest as he went to the wall. When he pushed the lever, something in the interior of the wall clicked, and the iron gate began to recede into the arch above.

He didn't look back as he passed beneath the iron bars and escaped into the world beyond.

FIVE

The castle was not even out of sight yet before Azreth's sense of triumph completely faded.

The landscape of the mortal realm assaulted him. Trees and waving grasses, two crescent moons, shifting white clouds, blinking stars. There was movement everywhere, drawing his attention in multiple directions at once, because there could be danger anywhere—how would he know? Everything here, absolutely everything, was new and different. He knew nothing except that he needed to keep moving.

He walked without thinking about his heading. His feet moved at a quickening tempo as his mind began to race.

He glanced down at the woman in his arms, who quickly looked away, her breath catching. She did not yet have the dead-eyed look that other mortal slaves had, but he supposed that she would eventually, if he kept her for long enough.

Could she tell that he had no idea what to do next?

The blood on his skin was cold and tacky, and as much as he'd enjoyed spilling it, he wanted it off. So he stopped when they came to a river, dumping the mortal onto her feet at its banks. Trusting that he could chase her if she ran—and that she had no way of seriously injuring him, even with the baton—he turned his back on her, pulled off his boots, and waded into the river.

Liquid bubbled around his knees. Instead of silky flames, freezing water gushed past. The cold didn't hurt him, but it was foreign and disquieting.

He rinsed the blood away and then scrubbed at the runes on his skin. The paint was stubborn. Scratching it furiously, he suppressed a frustrated snarl. He comforted himself by remembering the sweet taste of Eunaios's blood.

He would not be owned. He would not be helpless. He would not be weak.

When he got to the runes on his palm, he paused. He'd cleaned off the paint, but something remained—a set of silvery runes, shimmering faintly with embedded magic. He held his hand under the water, and they still wouldn't come off. His stomach turned.

Some part of the binding spell had stuck. He'd interrupted the ritual too late.

What had they done to him?

"What is your name?"

The woman's tentative voice startled him. He'd almost forgotten she was there. He turned to her, closing his hand to hide the marks from her.

What was his name? What a strange thing for her to ask, of all things.

"Do you have one?" she asked. Her face appeared open, earnest, even through the smeared makeup.

Mortals truly believed demonkind to be nothing more than dumb beasts, didn't they? His kind might not have been as clever with things like magic and technology as mortals were, but they were not animals.

"All sapient beings have names," he replied curtly.

She gave the tiniest of nods. "I am Raiya."

He knew that already. He'd heard the others call her by that name. But he didn't want to think about her name.

He recalled the hot, rich taste of her skin and blood when he'd pressed his tongue to her fingers. The serpent that was his hunger began to uncoil, and he waded toward her.

The mortal stayed completely still as he approached, either frozen with fear or impressively brave. Azreth touched her throat, and her fear spiked deliciously. Finally, she became unfrozen, and she fought him as he pulled her to the ground.

"Wait—" She flinched as he lowered himself over her, and then he missed whatever else happened to her expression, because his face was buried in her hair, her body, her neck, inches from a fluttering pulse that he could cut short if he just bit her there. Her heated distress washed over him, awful and wonderful. He held himself against the length of her, maximizing his contact to her body. Every part of her bled energy. It seeped into him like a vital tonic, like the essence of life itself, intoxicating and invigorating.

He felt dizzy with it—and with relief. He had dreamed of this kind of power and safety all his life. As long as he kept her, he would never have to wonder when his next meal would come... or whether it would come at all. He would never have to endure starvation and weakness for lack of a feeding source. With her, he could feed indefinitely. He could not just survive, but thrive.

Her small hands were pressed flat against his chest, trying to push him away, and she whimpered quietly. It was tragic. He couldn't imagine being so helpless.

His lips parted as he considered biting her, not deeply enough to kill her, but enough to hurt. His mouth hovered over her shoulder for long seconds, but he didn't move.

Trying to ignore her rapid breaths, he closed his eyes. He thought of the joy he'd felt when he'd torn through Eunaios and Nirlan's guards, and he concentrated on recapturing that feeling, thinking of death and blood and sated hunger. He waited for that excitement to come again as he thought of sinking his teeth into the woman.

Nothing happened. All he felt was unease.

Perhaps he could work her into a lustful state, instead. Then he would not have to physically hurt her. If mortals were anything like demons, she would give in to pleasure eventually, whether she wanted to or not. She wouldn't like it, but she would survive, just like he always had.

A sour taste filled the back of his throat. His skin itched and he began to sweat, and his breath was coming faster, and he didn't know why this sickness always came at the most inopportune times, times when he *most needed to focus.*

He needed her. There was no point in putting off the inevitable. If he was going to make her his slave, he should begin now. This was what his kind were meant to do, and what the mortals expected of them. The mortals would do the same to him if their positions were reversed. He would enjoy it; he'd never met a demon who wouldn't.

He had to do what was necessary to survive, just like every other demon. He could not be this weak. He just had to hold her still and—

His head pounded. His vision swam. He was going to vomit.

"Are you quite finished?" the human asked quietly.

Azreth pulled back to look at her. Her voice was filled with subtle venom, her expression disdainful. Suddenly, he missed the gentleness with which she'd asked his name.

Embarrassment was a foolish, pointless emotion, but he felt it anyway. He moved away from her and sat down beside the river to try to slow his breathing.

He was weak. He knew, deep down, that he would never not be weak. He'd been born this way. It was why the eldress had rejected him after she'd created him. She'd known, even then, that there was something wrong with him.

The woman shuddered with cold and reached into her bag to take out a dark gray blanket, which she threw around her shoulders. "How often do you have to do that—feed?"

"I am always hungry. And your smell is enticing."

"Do you plan to return to the hells now?"

"No."

She hesitated, her face grim. "Are you going to kill me?"

He saw no reason to lie to her. He wanted to keep her afraid, but not so afraid that she became desperate. "No."

"Why?"

Because he needed her to last.

Because she'd saved him.

When he didn't answer her, she asked, "Should I consider myself your prisoner?"

"Yes."

She paused, perhaps processing whatever emotions she was feeling about that. "What will you do now?"

She took a slow step toward him, trying too hard to be subtle, and his nerves prickled. He shot to his feet.

"I know you have a weapon. You should not attempt to use it." He sensed her fear rising enticingly again. He went to her, taking her arm in his hand. She stared at him intently, her mouth a straight, stubborn line, as he slowly raised her wrist to his nose and inhaled her scent. She smelled... so good.

She was nothing like the kin he'd fed from. Her emotions, and her mortal body for that matter, were full and lovely in a way he found difficult to put into words. She was filled with life, filled with feeling. Perhaps this was the trade-off for mortals—the forces of creation had squeezed more vitality into their short lifespans in exchange for decay and then death after a century or so.

He closed his eyes, letting his lips touch her palm. Magic

almost seemed to pass between them where they touched. Maybe, if he could just be near her, just like this, that would be enough...

"What if I stayed with you willingly?" she said in a nervous rush.

Azreth snapped out of his reverie. The woman was looking up at him apprehensively, her eyes darting to his teeth.

"I'll let you... use my body. To feed from. I won't fight you, and I won't try to escape."

He stared at her. He must have misunderstood.

"You will give yourself willingly?" he repeated.

"Yes. With some caveats."

"What caveats?"

She took a breath. "I don't want to be physically hurt. I don't want to be bruised or bloodied. I don't want to be forced. But I'll do my best to... satisfy you, otherwise."

Mortals didn't do this. He'd never heard of such a thing. "Why would you agree to this?"

"Because you can offer me something in exchange. I want you to protect me from my husband."

"Your husband?"

"Nirlan. The one who summoned you."

"He is your... your mate?"

"Yes."

He just looked at her, searching for signs of deception. He didn't know what mortals were like. He didn't know how to read her. She was not in league with Nirlan, though—that much was clear.

Was it possible that she really did see Azreth as her best option?

For a moment, he pictured her supine beneath him, gasping in the throes of pleasure, both defenseless and willing, as if she really desired him despite their differences. He frowned. "No one willingly submits to a demon. The only mortals willing to deal with my kind are the ones like your master. Those mortals only summon us when they know they can make us submit."

"I don't want to control you. I don't want to be controlled, either. Neither of us has to submit to the other as long as we stick to our agreement. We could be equals."

"Equals?"

She reached out, looking him in the eyes. To his shock, she slid her fingers into the waist of his sarong.

He jolted away reflexively. Grabbing her wrist, he bared his teeth. "You will touch me only when I grant you permission."

Her eyes widened. "Of course. I'm sorry."

His entire body felt flushed from surprise and discomfort. His heart was racing. He should not have let her catch him off guard. He was grateful no one else was there to witness him cringing away from a small human.

Frustrated by her strangeness, he said again, to make certain she understood, "Do not touch."

"I'm sorry. I didn't know. I won't do it again." Her eyes were large and clear, their dark centers piercing him. He got the sense that those eyes saw much, knew much.

"You want... an alliance."

"Yes," she said, as if it were that simple.

They could never be true allies. She would happily kill him if she had the chance, harmless though she may seem. Mortals had ways of turning the tides. If she could find a bit of iron and catch him unaware, she could end him as easily as he could her. He could never let his guard down. Not for a moment.

But deep down, he was relieved.

"You are wise to make this offer," he said flatly. "I agree to your terms."

She seemed to relax. "Will you tell me your name, then, since we're allies?"

"My name is Azreth," he said absently, looking at the grassy slopes around them again.

There was a strange enchantment marking his hand, and the human lord might be following him, and he needed to find someplace where he'd be safe. But she had been shivering and stumbling since he'd put her down. She must have needed rest. He'd heard that mortals needed a lot of it. "Mortals must sleep every night and eat every day," he said.

Her dark eyebrows came together in a question. "Yes...?"

"Then we must allow you time to rest, and then we must find you food to eat. Sleep now."

"Now?"

"Yes. It is night." Mortals slept at night. He knew that much.

She crossed her arms tightly, looking around. "I need to find a safe, warm place before I can sleep. It's too cold out here."

Even the mortals didn't like the chill of their own plane? Who was it for, then?

They were such delicate creatures. What other allowances would he need to make for her to be sure she stayed in good health?

He didn't want to risk giving off smoke that might be seen for miles, nor did he have any materials to build a warm shelter for her.

Reluctantly, he pulled her toward him and sat down on the cold ground. Her eyes were bright and wary, but she allowed him to pull her into his lap.

"You must stay with me. You will be warm enough." He braced his arms around her and pulled her against his chest. Her body felt cool; it barely gave off any heat. He hoped this would be enough. He truly knew nothing about how to survive in this place, and the longer he spent here, the more uncertain he became.

"Oh," she said softly.

He tilted his head toward her, narrowing his eyes. "Turn on me, and I will destroy you," he reminded her, lest she get too comfortable and think otherwise.

She sighed and said nothing.

"Now... go to sleep." He waited, watching her.

She blinked a few times, glanced up at him, then resolutely closed her eyes and didn't open them again. She let her head tilt to lay on his chest, but she did so hesitantly, as if his skin might be poisonous. Perhaps he just disgusted her, which would pose a problem if she really intended for him to pleasure her in order to feed.

They sat in silence for an hour or more, neither of them acknowledging the other, and neither of them sleeping.

Eventually, her breathing slowed, and her head grew heavier. Her fists uncurled. Azreth looked down with only his eyes, careful not to jostle her. Her expression had gone slack, the muscles of her face toneless in sleep.

Pale makeup still covered her face, a shield against his gaze, and her hair was tied back in a thick braid. Nearly her entire body was covered by clothing. She wore an elegant robe with a collar that crossed neatly at her chest and was belted at the waist, its blue color a little lighter and a little greener than his skin. Beneath that, she wore a long-sleeved shirt and long, loose trousers. It all looked more designed for comfort than defense.

He stared at her, feeling like a voyeur as he did so. It was the first time he'd witnessed another person sleeping. He had always thought a sleeping person might look a bit like a corpse, but he'd been wrong. She looked very alive and very relaxed, her entire body soft and at ease.

Holding her with one arm, he slowly reached for the bag she'd tucked by her feet, then peered inside. It was mostly empty. Apparently her blanket had taken up most of the space before she'd removed it. But there was also a book. He was intrigued. Books were where mortals stored knowledge.

He flipped through the pages. It was handwritten in a rather disorganized way, like the knowledge was still in progress, and there were several different scripts. He couldn't read any of them—the magic that gave him knowledge of other languages didn't extend to writing—but he recognized the distinctive shapes of the enchanting runes he'd seen all over the dungeon. The back of his neck prickled, and he glanced at the woman. She was still sleeping.

Reaching inside the bag again, he cautiously sorted through more cloth, some small jars, and a waterskin, and then his hand brushed something sharp and metallic. A weapon?

He pulled out the item to look at it, but its purpose became no clearer to him. It was a slender piece of metal about the length of his forefinger. The end had been sharpened to a severe point, but it didn't look especially ergonomic for stabbing.

Looking at the pointed end, he was suddenly reminded of the runes on the baton that was still attached to her belt. He looked down, studying the tiny runes carved on the baton's shaft. Tiny carvings required a tiny carving implement, he supposed. It was a stylus, not for writing, but for enchanting.

Who was this person he'd just stolen?

He silently put her things back inside her bag and rested it at her feet again. He didn't dare move from beneath her, even long after his legs had gone numb.

SIX

EIGHT YEARS AGO

zreth's boots pounded the dry earth as he gave chase across the wastes of the fourth hell.

It had been weeks since he'd fed. Hunger was eating him from the inside out. His mind was unwinding.

When a scrawny, turquoise-skinned demon had wandered through his path, it had felt like an act of mercy from the universe. Azreth had approached him, raising a hand in a solemn greeting. But the demon hadn't given him a chance to speak. As soon as he'd seen Azreth, he'd turned on his heel and taken off in a sprint.

Startled and annoyed, Azreth had run after him.

Azreth's legs were longer. He closed the distance between them quickly. When the smaller demon stumbled, Azreth tackled him from behind, and they crashed to the ground in a jumble of flailing limbs.

The demon beat against Azreth with hard fists and elbows, furious but mostly ineffectual. He was short and skinny, which was probably why he was alone. He'd been cast out, like Azreth, for being flawed. Now that they were face to face, Azreth could sense that he was young—maybe only a few weeks old—but he would never grow any larger. Kin were unlike mortals in that way. They were born as they were, and that was that. They could not change. The small demon wouldn't survive long, but through no fault of his own. The universe was unfair and unforgiving in its chaos. He had just been born unlucky, like Azreth.

The scent of his panic and anger was driving Azreth mad with hunger, but he didn't enjoy watching him struggle. Seeing the pain and fear in him made Azreth feel pain and fear, too, somehow.

He had never attacked someone in order to feed before. Usually, he was the one running away. He had chased instinctively, but now that he'd caught his prey, he feared what came next.

It was pathetic. His reluctance to feed was an insult to his race. Was he really so weak-willed that he would put someone else's well-being above his own? The universe had given him a smaller demon to take down and feed from—if he threw that away, then he deserved starvation.

"I will not hurt you," Azreth growled. "Be still." He lifted his hand away from one of the demon's wrists and brought it to the center of the demon's body, near his groin. He watched the demon's face, waiting for him to understand and, hopefully, stop panicking.

The turquoise demon hissed, then—of all things—gave an angry sob. "I don't want this. Let go of me."

It was such a strange, *emotional* reaction that Azreth drew back, repelled.

As Azreth hesitated, the demon bent his knee and kicked him in the face. Azreth didn't bother to strike back. The demon scrambled to his feet and ran, and for reasons beyond understanding, Azreth was glad that he did. He put a hand to his jaw as he watched the turquoise demon disappear into the dunes. The bone felt cracked.

He remembered being young and frightened, too. He remembered how much he'd hated it. But he hadn't cried or begged. What would have been the point?

This was just the way things were. It was what their kind were made to do. What they were *supposed* to do.

He tried to recall whether he'd ever demanded to be released by a demon who had subdued him. But of course he hadn't. It wouldn't have occurred to him. He'd fought, of course—that was the one thing he would always do. But he'd never sobbed in outrage or protested at what was done to him.

It was right that people who were strong enough to overpower him could do as they liked with him. It was what he'd deserved. It was the inevitable result of his own weakness. So of course he'd never done something as foolish as protest it.

I don't want this? What did it matter what he wanted? Why did he think he deserved better than the rest of them?

The longer he thought about it, the angrier he became.

The turquoise demon was arrogant. And it was a shame Azreth hadn't killed him for it.

Disquieted, angry, and still hungry, he carefully healed his jaw and kept walking.

SEVEN

It continued getting colder throughout the night, and Azreth found himself glad for the mild warmth of the woman's body blanketing him.

When the sun began to rise, it cast the mortal realm in gray-blue light. The colors here were all wrong; the sky was cold and icy blue, and that color melted down onto everything else in this world.

It was surprisingly quiet. Calm. Some small creatures stirred—tiny insects and birds, and once, a strange rodent ran by. He watched them all warily, wondering if any were venomous, but they did not bother him—or the woman.

After many hours, she stirred again. Her eyes blinked open, and she looked momentarily alarmed to find herself in his arms, as if she'd forgotten what had happened the previous day. She clambered out of his lap and took a step away from him, eager to put space between them.

"I must feed now," he said softly. There was no point in putting off the inevitable. If she wasn't willing to hold up her end of their agreement, it would be better to find out sooner than later.

Her face hardened, but she nodded. She went to the river to wash, first. Azreth turned away, looking out at the vast blue-green-gold plains. It felt like she was delaying what came next, and that didn't bode well.

When she returned, her makeup was gone, her face damp. He was startled to see a faint bruise beneath her eye.

"You're injured," he said, stupidly.

"It's nothing. I can perform just fine, I promise."

He frowned, remembering the rough way he'd handled her in his cell when Nirlan had thrown her to him. "Did I do that to you when they put you in my cage?"

"You don't remember?"

He couldn't answer. Things from that day were hazy.

"No," she said eventually. "This was my husband."

Azreth considered that. Her husband had attacked her, and that was why she had resorted to allying with a demon instead? Or perhaps she was the one who had attacked Nirlan, and he had only been defending himself.

Looking closer, he saw a line of scratches on her throat leading beneath the collar of her robe. He reached out and folded the edge of the collar down, following the trail of marks. They grew darker and deeper beneath her clothes. Azreth had a flash of memory suddenly, recalling his hand clawing over her throat. He quickly let go of her.

"I have heard that mortals only take willing mates," he said.

"Usually."

"Did your husband force you into marriage?"

Her eyes flashed, but her voice was quiet. "No, he didn't force me."

"So you formed an alliance with him, agreed to be equals, and now you have betrayed him."

The look she gave him was definitely defiant, now. "Yes, I suppose I have."

Her honesty was impressive. Her lack of loyalty, less so. At least he knew exactly how much to trust her now. "I must feed," he repeated.

She shifted and glanced away. "What do I need to do?"

"Arouse yourself."

She actually scoffed, as if it were a ridiculous request. "I can't. Just... just do what you want with me."

He was torn between annoyance and interest. Hesitantly, fully expecting her to snarl and bite him, he stepped closer and raised a hand toward her face.

"Remember our agreement," she said.

"You do not want to be bruised, or bloodied, or forced."

She seemed surprised that he remembered.

Cautiously, he touched her cheek. Her skin was slightly warm, but cooler than he'd expected, much cooler than any demon's. And it was soft. Velvety. Pillowy. Addictive. She stood perfectly still, watching him in a way that seemed faintly judgmental.

He had only ever touched other living beings during feeding exchanges like he'd had with Nariel, or during fights to the death. No one had ever given him the freedom to examine the heat and texture and shape of their body. It felt wrong, or unfair, like he was taking something from her. Which he supposed he was—that was the whole point of this.

He could give her pleasure, though, if she allowed it. Of this, he was confident. To the kin, giving pleasure was like breathing.

He let his hand drift down her throat to her chest, flattening his palm gently over her heart, which was beating quickly. He frowned a little, but he continued, slipping his hand beneath the crossed collar of her robe. She stiffened, giving off a flare of fear and anger. His frown deepened, and he pulled away from her.

She detested him. And why shouldn't she? He was coercing her.

"What?" she asked, as if they didn't both know.

"You said you would be willing." It came out as a growl, which seemed cruel, because this entire situation was his fault. She had not asked for this, not exactly.

"I'm trying," she said. "Keep going."

Determined, he reached for her again—and he just as quickly lost his determination. The scent of her fear and hatred should have aroused his predator's instinct, but it just sickened him. He felt nauseous, too hot, his heart beating too hard.

He couldn't just let her go. He needed to feed from her, or he needed to feed from some other mortal, but he needed to feed. In a burst of frustration, he snapped, "If you cannot do this, then you must find someone else who will."

"I can do it," she insisted. Her eyes fell to his waist just for a moment before snapping away again. "I could... use my mouth?"

It took him several seconds to understand what she was suggesting.

Did she actually think he'd let someone put their teeth near him? And did she think he could feed from his own passion?

Did she really just not understand what he needed from her?

"That is not how it works," he said.

"Then how does it work?"

"The energy I feed on comes from others. From you. My body is not relevant. Only yours matters."

She blinked at him.

"Do you know how to pleasure yourself?" he asked.

"Of course I do."

"Then do it."

She thought for a moment. The scent of her fear began to fade. "Do you need to watch me?"

With other demons, he usually touched during feeding, but he supposed it wasn't strictly necessary. If this was what she needed, it would be a small sacrifice to make. "No. But I must be nearby."

She seemed to relax a great deal. She was relieved that he wouldn't touch her or look at her.

She went to the other side of a large stone nearby. Having her out of his line of sight made him nervous, but he suppressed the urge to chase after her. He put his back to the stone, and he waited.

There was a long pause during which nothing happened. Azreth sat very still, tense.

And then, he felt something. Though she was out of sight, he knew the moment she began. There was a prick of heat in the air, thin and frail, but it was there.

Slowly, the heat grew. Her pleasure drifted to him in soft, pink breezes, heady and untainted by fear.

It was unexpectedly lovely.

Perhaps he shouldn't have been surprised, because every other aspect of humans had been delicious, too. He simply hadn't expected to be so affected by it. He closed his eyes, letting it soak into him.

Without really meaning to, he imagined what she might look like at that moment—her flushed face turned toward the sky, eyes closed, breasts tight, inner thighs coated in wetness.

When she reached her peak, there was a burst of ecstasy that had his eyes rolling back. The pleasure that surrounded him satisfied his hunger, but it also made his cock twitch. He was half hard beneath his sarong, to his dismay. He didn't usually become aroused without the help of magic, and he preferred it that way. He disliked the idea of a part of his body acting without his consent. Swallowing tightly, he stood.

Sex was a means to an end. It was a necessary part of life that was usually unpleasant, if tolerable. He did not *like* sex.

But he liked imagining the mortal like this—lush, beautiful, eager.

He heard a hurried rustling, then she came around the stone to meet him, breathing a little faster than usual. Her face was flushed, just like he'd imagined. She looked up at him questioningly.

She'd fed him. She'd done it willingly, and he hadn't had to harm her. It had been so simple, so painless. For the first time since he'd left the hells, he felt a flicker of hope.

Raiya was still looking up at him, waiting for him to say something.

"Good," he said stiffly.

She lowered her head, but her eyes lingered on him, darting over his chest, his arms, his waist. Her blush deepened.

EIGHT

Azreth did not want to ask the mortal for advice on where to go, so he just went in the opposite direction of the castle. He needed to keep moving. Fear always set in worst when you stopped moving. As long as you were running faster than everyone else, no one could hurt you.

Raiya had not eaten since they'd left the castle. She'd brought nothing with her in her little bag, and Azreth had nothing of his own to offer her.

"How often do you eat?" he asked her.

She jerked a little, startled by his voice, and she fingered the end of her braided hair. "Three times a day, usually."

Azreth was dumbfounded. Mortal bodies were beyond his comprehension. She needed to eat thrice every single day? Was she already fading, then, after not having had a morning meal? How long would she last without feeding? Would she even make it to the end of the day?

He'd had no idea just how fragile humans were before he'd met her. It worried him. He didn't know how to find things like food or shelter on this plane. But he was the one who'd taken her from the safety of her home, away from those things, so he was responsible for her health now.

He was relieved when he saw a single small dwelling perched atop a broad, low hill in the distance. The structure was simple, made of organic materials, nothing like the stone fortress Raiya had lived in. It was completely alone in the vast landscape, undefended.

"Where are you going?" Raiya asked as he turned toward the building.

"There is a house. We will find food there."

Raiya's steps faltered. He glanced down at her, sensing a dark emotion brewing in her. "Wait. I don't think that's wise."

"Why not?"

"What if there's someone inside?"

He lifted an eyebrow at her. It was unlikely that a mortal commoner or two would pose a threat to them. They wouldn't try to hurt her while she was with him. But if they did— "I will kill them," he assured her.

Her eyes widened. "No! Stay here and let me go alone. Please." She ran in front of him, forcing him to stop.

He had thought she might be glad that he'd been thinking of her needs. Apparently not.

Quite the opposite, in fact. She wanted to leave him here while she ran inside to scheme with the other mortals. Maybe she thought they would help her escape him, or even kill him. He could think of no other reason for her sudden urgency. And he'd already witnessed her opportunistic nature first-hand, when she'd asked him to kill Nirlan.

Scowling, he stepped around her and kept walking. "You will stay with me."

"But—"

"*No.*"

Raiya went silent. After a moment, he heard her following him.

There was a lone human working in the field outside the house. As they approached, the man looked up and stared. He was as small and thin as all the other mortals Azreth had seen, his scant muscles hidden by a layer of soft fat. The man made a strangled sound, then turned and ran inside, slamming the door behind him.

By the time Azreth got to the door, whoever was inside the house had gone quiet.

He hesitated, unexpectedly nervous.

It was just a house. There would only be mortals inside, and he could kill them just as easily as he had the guards at the castle. But the last time he'd underestimated mortals, he'd almost died in a cage. Fear had infiltrated his mind like a sickness.

He clenched his jaw. He was strong. This plane would not kill him. He could not let it.

He pushed on the door, but it didn't move. Something was blocking it from the other side. In a controlled thrust, he drove his fist into the wood. It shattered easily.

Someone inside the house screamed in fear, which bolstered his confidence. He broke the door into pieces and pushed the remnants aside, then stepped over the threshold.

Immediately, there were more screams. He narrowed his eyes as he adjusted to the dim interior. The several humans inside scattered away from the door, pressing themselves against walls as far away from him as possible. None of them wore armor or carried weapons. Azreth watched their wide eyes trace up his body and over his horns, which were bumping against the ceiling. Bits of thatch tore loose whenever he turned his head.

They were terrified. He felt a peculiar combination of relief and unease. He wasn't used to being stared at.

He looked around the room—for the entire house was just one single room. It was the warmest place he'd been since coming to this chilly plane. Along one wall was a space dedicated to cooking, with a fire and food storage. Something boiled noisily inside a pot.

He had heard that mortals had odd food preferences, and that they liked to boil many different carcasses and plants together into a sludge. It smelled of meat, but also of other unfamiliar and unpleasant herbal and vegetal ingredients. He wondered if they were toxic.

He heard Raiya's feet padding carefully over the broken door behind him. Just as he started toward the cooking area, something hit him in the back, almost hard enough to hurt.

He spun to face her, but it wasn't Raiya who had struck him. Beside her was a young man holding a shovel—the same small man they'd seen outside, who was now looking like he severely regretted what he'd just done.

How had Azreth forgotten about the man already? He should have counted the occupants of the house. He should have made certain he knew where all of his enemies were, including any lurking behind him. If it had been another demon instead of a mortal, such a foolish mistake would have cost him his life.

Annoyed, he jerked the shovel from the man's hands and threw it across the room. The house was made of brittle wood, and the blade of the shovel stuck in the wall like a dart.

Instead of cowing them like he'd expected, this only seemed to spur the mortals into action. From his other side, there was a rush of footsteps as someone approached, and then something hit him.

He cried out as agony pulsed through him. It siphoned the strength from his body, making his legs shake and his vision blacken. He looked down, and dread filled him. A long, metal bar protruded from his side. Its rough surface had made a jagged rip in his skin, tearing instead of cutting.

Iron.

It was like acid, like teeth, like razors and ice inside him. Soon he'd be on his knees, perhaps unconscious, perhaps dead. His summoned arm flickered as he struggled to maintain concentration on the spell.

He grabbed the stick of iron. The surface of it touching his hand was like frostbite, and he fought the instinct to immediately let go. Sharp, liquid pain burst across his fingers and up his arm. His hand shook.

With a jerk and a cry, he wrenched it out and threw it far away. Blood poured from his side, his natural healing slowed by the poisonous metal. The mortals were screaming and shouting and darting around him in panic. Their emotions were so thick that they were almost suffocating. He shook his head, struggling to keep his senses straight.

They would attack with iron again. He had to stop them now.

He lashed out half blindly, knocking the younger man across the room, then he grabbed the man who'd stabbed him and raised him into the air. Dark emotions vibrated throughout the room, sinking into him in invigorating waves. The mortal stared into his eyes. There was utter hatred in the man's face right alongside the fear.

Azreth had been a fool to lower his guard. Mortals were just as vicious as demons, just as filled with hate, just as devious and self-serving.

Something was weakly but insistently pulling at his arm. "Azreth," said a voice that seemed oddly distant though the sound of blood pulsing in his ears. "Azreth!"

Dragging his attention away from the man, Azreth looked down. Raiya was at his side, her small hands wrapped around his arm and tugging at him as hard as they could. She flinched when he looked down at her, as if she thought he would strike her next.

Her expression was desperate and filled with worry. She wasn't trying to fight him—she was begging.

"They're just afraid!" she cried. "They're only farmers. Please let them go!"

Let them go?

She made it sound as if he were holding them hostage. He had been perfectly willing to leave them alone before they attacked him.

A piercing wail cut through the air, and Azreth started. It was unlike anything he'd ever heard. The sound was coming from a bundle of cloth in the arms of the woman huddled against the wall. To his shock, he saw a tiny, scrunched-up face within the bundle, like a little fat grub with a human face. It was screaming.

It was a human baby. He stared at it, disconcerted. The sound it made was a perfect natural defense mechanism. It would have been defenseless otherwise, being so small and soft, but he would have done nearly anything to get away from that sound.

The mother was crying silently, and when Azreth looked her way, she clutched the baby tighter against her chest to shield it from his gaze. He'd seen the same behavior in animals in the hells. A nyra would defend her hatchlings even at the cost of her own life.

The idea of being so small and helpless, completely dependent upon others for survival, was so horrible he could hardly bear to think about it.

It was then that he noticed several of the other humans were too small to be fully grown, too. This was a mortal family. A wife and husband and their children. After Raiya's interruption, they'd stopped attacking him and had gone back to cowering and screaming.

For a moment, he imagined what another demon might

have done in his place. He thought of the man in his hands ripped in half lengthwise until his guts unraveled to the floor. He thought of the baby pulled from its bundle and smashed against the stone hearth. He thought of the mother screaming while her children were killed slowly. He imagined how their pain would taste. He tried, experimentally, to find the thoughts appealing.

It didn't work. The sounds of their cries grated on him like claws on slate.

He did not enjoy being the cause of this suffering. It did not give him the same pleasure he'd felt when he'd torn through the castle. He did not like this.

He didn't like that he didn't like it.

Raiya stood in front of him, lifting her hands placatingly. She spoke to him the way one might speak to a large, frightening, and not-very-intelligent beast. "They were afraid you would hurt them. They can do you no harm. You don't have to do this. Please. Please, don't kill them."

Before he had come to this plane, he had imagined that he would enjoy hearing mortals beg him for mercy. But he found that he disliked this, as well.

He glanced up at the man he was still holding aloft. The man looked back with a pained grimace.

Slowly, Azreth lowered him to the floor. As soon as his feet touched the floor, the man backed away, stopping near the wailing infant. Azreth wondered if he meant to protect the child, or if he just hoped the horrible sound would ward Azreth away from them both.

Shaken, Azreth looked at them all as they stared at him. Gritting his teeth, he pressed a hand to the wound at his side, which was still bleeding freely and hurt like all the hells. He could still feel the taint of the iron inside him.

The pot on the fire boiled over suddenly, hissing.

In all the confusion, he'd almost forgotten what they'd

come here for. Giving the humans a warning glance, he went to the cooking space.

He scanned the bizarre assortment of items resting on the table and on shelves along the wall: bundles of absurdly tiny leaves, jars of some kind of rotten-smelling paste, other jars filled with yellow and red and black dirt, ugly bulbous roots, a large knife that had been set down in the middle of carving those roots into immaculate little squares...

He was annoyed and overwhelmed by it all. Everything in the mortal realm was inexplicable. What was all of this for? What possible need could they have for such excess? Why were mortals so ridiculous? Why had this endeavor—feeding a single small human—become so complicated?

He impatiently grabbed a large, skinned piece of meat still attached to the bone, because it smelled the least bad out of everything, before stalking to the door.

"Human," he snapped at Raiya, motioning outside. After a moment, he heard her following.

NINE

She trailed after him quietly as he hurried away from the house on the hill. He didn't know where he was going, except that he was getting away from the house, and he was doing it quickly.

Several hills later, he could still feel Raiya's eyes on his back. Fearing him. Despising him. Looking down on him.

He didn't understand anything about this plane. He'd never thought the people in the house would try to fight him. It was a ridiculous, irrational thing to do. How could he have anticipated that?

Maybe it was not possible to predict what mortals would do. They were too strange to him, too different from demons.

He came to a stop and looked down at Raiya. She looked back at him, her face still and thoughts hidden.

She'd tried to stop him from going into that house. Perhaps he should have listened to her. He might not be able to trust her motives, but he could trust that she knew more about this plane than he did.

Setting down the meat he'd taken from the house, he put a hand to his side and began healing his iron-burned wound.

"Iron is poisonous to you, isn't it?" Raiya said. "That's why you couldn't lift the portcullis with your hands."

His spellcasting hand went still. He looked into her eyes, trying to see through them into her mind. She just looked at his wound, her face crinkling slightly, like she didn't like the look of it.

"Are you all right?" she asked. Her expression was neutral, her tone soft. For once, there was no fear coming from her while she looked at him. If she were a demon, he would assume she was on the lookout for weakness. Weakness in him would be an opportunity for her to attack.

"It is a flesh wound," he said finally. Raiya just arched an eyebrow.

When he told her to eat the meat, she refused, saying that it needed to be heated on a fire first, or she would get sick from it. At that point, he suspected she might be making things up just to toy with him, but he didn't know enough about humans to be certain she was lying, and he couldn't risk getting her ill. So he quietly made her a fire, feeling foolish as he did so.

After the meat was heated, she chewed dainty, steaming pieces without complaint, finally. Azreth watched her eat, and the nervous coils in the pit of his stomach slowly unfolded. They would survive another day.

"Will you explain something to me?" Raiya's voice was cautious, but her eyes were daring. "I always thought demons came to our plane because they were mindless creatures hell-bent on tormenting mortals. But you are far from mindless, and you haven't tormented me, at least. So why do you not return to the hells? Heilune is dangerous for your kind."

Heilune. He turned the word over in his mind. It was the name of this land, he realized, all the way from one ocean to the other, encompassing many mortal races and landscapes.

He stood up, pacing around the fire as she finished eating.

"Whatever awaits me in Heilune, it is better than what I left behind."

She leaned forward. "What is it like there? I have studied much of this world, but not much is known about yours."

He tried to recall the last time someone had talked to him as much as she did. Even Nariel, who he'd thought was quite a social creature, didn't ask him questions like this.

He thought of Nariel. The eldresses. The endless red dunes he'd become lost in too many times, and the skeletal trees he'd butchered to make tools and shelters. The venomous blossoms and spiked vines, the slithering beasts he'd had to keep watch for when he went to bathe in the rivers of fire, the wind storms that could blow the skin from your bones. It was all so different from the cool greenness of this plane.

What was it like? He didn't know where to start. He didn't know how to explain it to her.

It was an unhappy place.

Avoiding her eyes, he picked up a stick and fidgeted with the fire. "We have talked enough about the hells," he said shortly, then gestured to her bag. "That book you have. There are runes in it."

Her lips parted in surprise, and then she frowned. "You searched my bag?"

"Yes. To help me decide whether you pose a threat to me."

"Oh? And am I a threat, in your estimation?"

Of course she was a threat to him. Allying with a mortal was one of the more dangerous things he'd ever done. But she knew that. She was mocking him.

"You know runes," he said. "You read the runes in the dungeon when they tried to bind me. That's how you knew how to break the mage's spell so thoroughly."

"Yes," she admitted.

"Are you a mage?"

Her frown deepened. "No. Nothing so glamorous."

He believed her. She probably would have used magic against him by now if she were capable of it.

He glanced surreptitiously at the shimmering runes staining his palm. He needed her help again, and he had to convince her to give it willingly, because he could not force her to be truthful.

"I would like to amend our agreement," he said carefully.

She looked suspicious. "How so?"

"I require assistance with this." He showed her the marks on his hand, and she studied them with great interest—possibly too much interest.

"I was too late," she said softly.

"What do they say?"

Tentatively, she reached toward his hand. Azreth stiffened as he realized she was going to touch him.

She put a slender finger to his palm. A prickle began beneath her finger and spread throughout his body, raising the hair on the back of his neck, and he resisted the urge to pull away. Raiya pointed to each of the runes one by one, explaining that they meant ominous things like "death" and "promise" and "forever," but he couldn't focus on anything but the odd sensation of her touch. Each soft, cool press of her fingertip sent a chill through him.

People in the hells grabbed each other, grappled, bit, and clawed, but they didn't touch each other like this.

"What do they do?" he asked.

She looked almost sympathetic. "I think it's a piece of a kind of soulbinding. A spell that will keep you partially bound to Nirlan."

Memories assaulted him. The cage in the castle. The feeling of his strength draining as he starved. Helplessness. Lord Nirlan's ugly, patronizing smile as he told Azreth what he envisioned for his future slavery.

He could not let that happen. He could not be helpless again.

"Bound in what way?" he asked.

"I'm not sure. It's half a spell. Since it was interrupted, I can't know for certain what the effects are. It could mean nothing... or it could mean that something bad will happen to you if you're away from Nirlan for too long."

"Can they be removed?"

"I'm not sure. There may be a way."

"Help me find one, and I will protect you from the mate you betrayed."

She looked annoyed, offended by the reminder of her betrayal. "You're already doing that, remember?"

He closed his hand into a fist, hiding the runes inside. He needed to convince her of his value, but he had little else to offer her. "I will protect you from any other dangers we cross," he said firmly. "I will ensure that you are fed and sheltered and healthy. I am strong and capable, even in this unfamiliar land. If you do this for me, I will destroy anyone who crosses you. You have my word."

She just raised her eyebrows, and Azreth feared he hadn't impressed her.

"Do you doubt my abilities?" he snapped.

To his surprise, she said, "No." It sounded like she was considering agreeing. It also sounded like she was thinking about something she wasn't saying aloud.

"You must uphold your end of the agreement," he reminded her. "Betray me, and I—"

"You will destroy me. Yes. I know." It had only been a day, and already she'd started mocking him when he tried to intimidate her. Maybe he'd been too gentle with her and she'd decided he was weak.

"You cannot outwit me," he said. "Plot against me, attempt to deceive me, and I will know."

To his dismay, she continued to ignore him, reaching into her bag to retrieve her book of runes and a writing stick. She began making notes, perfectly calm and composed. "I would have helped you regardless of our agreement. I don't need anything extra in exchange. No one deserves to be enslaved."

He stared at her. If it was a lie, it was a bold one, but he didn't think it could be the truth, either. Maybe she was making a joke he didn't understand.

"But if you want my help, there are a few other conditions you must agree to," she said.

Azreth frowned. "You said you didn't need anything."

"These things are not for me." She put the book away and looked up at him, reproachful. "You can't barge into places where you're not welcome. If you don't want to end up on the end of a Paladin's sword, you must listen to me."

He scoffed. "I will not lie down for those who bear weapons against me."

"Then don't break into their houses and steal from them." Her tone made it sound like she'd barely restrained herself from adding, *"You imbecile,"* at the end of the sentence. "I won't help you if it means bullying people weaker than you. I've spent too much time around bullies of late."

Azreth thought about that word, *bully*. The demon gift of language let him understand its meaning, but he could think of no analogous word in the demonic language.

Did mortals believe it was wrong to use your strength to your advantage? Did they not love power and abhor weakness the way his kind did, then?

That was why she'd protected the family in the house, he realized. There had been no other benefit for her. She simply believed it was wrong to hurt them.

"I have no desire to hurt the weak," he said honestly.

Raiya paused, studying him. "Well... Good."

She took a circle of silver out of her bag—a bracelet. "I was going to use this when I left Nirlan, but you should probably take it. It's a simple glamour. It will help you blend in with mortals. It won't make you invisible, but it should be able to alter your appearance enough to keep people from attacking you on sight."

It was a bright, shiny metal. If there was any iron in it, it was not enough for him to sense it, but it was covered in tiny, dark runes.

"It needs to be charged with magic first," Raiya added. "I've never actually used it before."

"I can charge it."

She looked down, uncomfortable. "Enchantments require quite a lot of magic."

She clearly knew what came next. Azreth felt a pang of regret at her discomfort. "Then I will need to feed," he said.

"Is there something that will give you more power than what I did before?" she asked. "Something that I'd actually be willing to do, I mean?"

"Stronger emotions are better. The easiest avenues to power are pain and sex. In the hells, demons often torture each other for it."

She gave a nervous smile. "That wouldn't be my first choice."

"It is not anyone's first choice."

"Then sex is easiest?"

"Yes. The effect would be greater if I touched you this time."

Something subtle scented the air between them. Raiya was feeling an anticipatory emotion he couldn't quite identify, but her face remained closed off. "Touch me how?"

"It doesn't matter. But being in close proximity to you will make the magic stronger. Even better if I am touching your skin."

She nodded once. "Then... let's do that."

TEN

The next part would be easier than talking. Pleasuring a mortal was something he knew how to do. It was something demons were instinctively skilled at—just like killing. He put his hands on her waist and pulled her closer.

Startled, she put her hands against him. "Wait."

She was not quite looking at him, like she was trying to imagine she was someplace else. Azreth's discomfort grew as he waited for her to steel herself. He understood the difficulty of needing to complete this task when you didn't want to.

He'd never expected to see so many of his own feelings reflected in a mortal. But then, he'd never spent much time thinking about their feelings before now.

Eventually, he sensed her nerves beginning to settle. She glanced up at him, waiting for him to continue. Her eyes were dark and hooded, and there was something unnerving about the blackness in their depths. He wondered if mortal eyes saw more than his own. What could she see when she looked at him?

He thought about how she'd touched his hand—so lightly, like the brush of a feather.

Moving very slowly this time, he sank to the ground, then guided her into his lap, putting her back to his front. She was stiff, leaning slightly away from him. Putting her in his lap only emphasized their size difference. Her legs were framed by his thighs, and her shoulders still came up below his. He waited, hoping she would relax. She didn't. She looked ahead, unmoving.

He was glad she had his back to him, because he didn't want her to look at him.

"You would like my assistance?" he asked, wondering if she'd changed her mind.

Raiya stiffened. "Yes. Please."

And then, despite everything, Azreth felt something heating the air between them. A flicker of lust. He might have missed it if he hadn't been paying attention.

"We may as well get it done with quickly," she added.

"Yes," he said uncertainly. He looked down over her shoulder, his eyes traveling down her bare neck to the scant triangle of her chest that was visible before the robe covered it. He could see nothing of the shape of her breasts, but he could imagine them, just as he could imagine the curves of her hips and thighs and the pale gold-brown of her smooth, clear skin beneath her clothes.

He realized, suddenly, that he found her beautiful.

Which was irrelevant. Mortals all served the same purpose. It didn't matter if he found them beautiful or not.

Testing the waters, he shifted his knee so that his thigh pressed between her legs. She drew in a breath, and her excitement and nerves bloomed in the air.

"Have you done this before?" she asked.

"Not with a mortal."

"Do you know what you're doing?"

"You will have to let me know." He reached beneath the split on the side of her robe, running his hand over her trousers and along the soft warmth of her inner thigh before grasping between her legs, conforming his hand to the curved shape of her sex.

Raiya tensed. Her eyes were closed now, her jaw tight with grim determination.

The last time he'd tried to feed from her while touching her, in his cage in the dungeon, he'd been out of control with hunger. It was no wonder she was afraid of him.

He wanted to show her how good he could be. He wanted to feed from her, but more than that, he found himself wanting to please her—which was an uncomfortably submissive desire, and he didn't quite know how to feel about it.

Conscious of her preference for a soft touch, he let his hand open and relax into the crux of her thighs. He watched her face closely as he eased his hand upward to the head of her arousal. She held her breath. Her hips cocked back, her thighs squeezing him. He studied her reactions to each measured touch, learning what increased her enjoyment and what didn't. He watched her lips slowly part as he cupped her in his hand.

She was brave. Azreth had never allowed someone to touch him like this.

In fact, he had never been given permission to touch someone without offering his own body in exchange, either. He had never had the opportunity to watch someone willingly twitch and writhe with pleasure from his ministrations.

He lifted her thigh with one hand, opening her legs further, and he felt a surge of triumph as she made a soft sound and leaned back against him for support. Arousal emanated from her, thick and heady.

To his frustration, his cock was stiffening again. It made

him nervous and angry. It made him feel weak. But he couldn't bring himself to stop.

He wondered if she had ever imagined coupling with him, even if it was only a fantasy she would never act upon. He pictured her shrugging off her robe to bare herself to him, lying on her back like Nariel never had, and parting her legs for him. Submitting to him. Wanting him.

Through their clothes, the head of his cock would not stop rubbing against her backside, and his resolve was weakening.

He bent his head, leaning into her warm hair. He imagined her inner channel softening under his touch, as if she would welcome him inside her. "You smell like lust," he murmured.

Perhaps it frightened her, because she half-heartedly pressed a hand to his thigh as if to put some distance between them, even as her pleasure flared. Instinctively, he pulled her tightly against him and redoubled his efforts on her sex. She made a faint sound as her hips bucked. His cock strained against her. He wanted to feel her skin, to sink into the heat between her legs, to watch her come undone on his fingers. He lifted his hand away from her body long enough to find the waist of her trousers and slide beneath it.

She gasped. "No. Wait."

He paused. "Why not?"

"I just—just please don't." She sounded desperate.

Azreth snapped out of the embarrassing fugue state of lust he'd entered. He looked down at Raiya, who was suddenly fearful and unhappy. She was afraid of being overpowered.

He had the perverse urge to try to comfort her. How one might do that, though, he had no idea. He'd never tried to comfort someone before, because that would be a strange and unnatural thing to do.

Grimacing with distaste at himself, he pulled his hand

away from the waist of her trousers and placed it on her thigh. "Be at ease," he murmured.

She exhaled, her head tipping back to rest on his shoulder, as if she really were put at ease. Or maybe the effort of trying to reach climax was just tiring her. Her emotions were heavy and convoluted, but he knew she was close.

He held her for a moment as he waited for the fear to recede. Then he eased his fingers along her inner thigh—courting her again. He brushed his thumb over her center. The lightness of the touch would drive anyone mad eventually. He waited for her to show him she was ready.

Only when she arched, pressing her body against his hand needily, did he begin to handle her in earnest again. A swell of pleasure came from her as his fingers pressed just beneath the crest of her sex.

"*There,*" she said breathlessly.

"I know." As if there was any chance he could have missed it. He dutifully continued in even, steady strokes until her entire body undulated, her fingers clutching at him as she reached her peak.

The essence of her poured into him, and he groaned, doubling over. It was a feast. It was ecstasy. For a moment, everything in the world was perfect and beautiful. Both of them gasped and trembled and moaned together in united bliss.

It was not mere copulation. It was not like Nariel. And he felt a deep regret as he realized there was no coming back from this. Nothing else would ever compare.

ELEVEN

zreth had never charged an enchantment before, but fortunately, it came naturally to him. It was like feeding in reverse. Raiya watched his hands as he worked on the bracelet, and there was a greedy glint in her eyes that he'd not seen in her before now. Ambition? Jealousy? Perhaps... admiration? A part of him was just relieved to see something other than quiet fear and resignation in her soul.

Her face was still flushed from earlier. His gaze dropped to her lips, which seemed plumper and redder than before. Her eyes darted up to his, and she shifted nervously when she realized she was being studied.

"Are mortals preferable to demons for feeding?" she asked. "Is that why your people come to Heilune? Because we... taste better?" She had many questions. The more time they spent together, the more she asked.

He turned the bracelet in his hands, wondering how he would know when it was finished charging. "They are preferable because they are soft and weak and easily frightened. Your plane is a feast for us."

"We are not weak."

He glanced at her.

"We're not weak," she repeated, narrowing her eyes.

He was surprised she was so defensive. She could see their physical differences just as easily as he could.

Then again, he wouldn't like being called weak either, and he didn't want to anger his only ally. He searched for a better way to put it.

"You are... not strong," he said, then he realized that wasn't quite right, either. There was more than one kind of strength. "Mortals are small and easy to break. They cannot put up much of a fight. It is different in the hells. We must fight every day in order to survive. That's why many try to make their way here, even when it comes with great risk. That, and you taste better." As he'd just discovered.

"Perhaps other demons would have an easier time if they all behaved like you. It isn't so bad being fed from when you do it like that."

He looked up at her so sharply that he almost dropped the bracelet. She gave a nervous smile and looked away, folding her arms tightly over her chest.

It isn't so bad being fed from when you do it like that.

A hot emotion, alive and vibrating like buzzing insects, filled his chest.

"Perhaps," he agreed. "Not everyone has such a willing donor on hand."

The bracelet began to resist his magic, and he got the sense it had drunk its fill. He held it out to Raiya. The runes, which had been dark and difficult to make out, now gleamed with subtle blue-green light.

Her face lit up as she admired their combined work: her runes, and his magic. "Put it on."

He almost did so, but stopped short. For all he knew, it

could have been enchanted with a spell that killed whoever donned it. He held it out to her. "You, first."

Her smile faded. She took the bracelet from him and slipped it over her wrist. "I can tell you are a man who does not trust easily, Azreth," she said dryly. And then her skin turned the exact same blue as his own—mocking him. He recoiled slightly. He did not particularly like mortals, but he liked other demons even less. Until that moment, he hadn't realized how much he appreciated her wholly un-demonic appearance.

She continued to change. Her skin and hair flashed violet and red and green and every other color imaginable before finally returning to her natural appearance.

The illusion was simple, but effective. He had not seen this kind of spell before. Demon magic tended to be less subtle and more focused on potential for violence. "It changes your coloring," he said.

"Yes, and it didn't even strike me dead in the process." She pulled it off and thrust it toward him.

The bracelet was dainty and narrow. Feeling overlarge and oafish, he carefully bent the stiff metal until it opened wide enough to fit around his wrist, then bent it closed again. He sensed the magic activate somehow, as though it knew he was there and was awaiting his instruction.

He glanced up at Raiya, using her as a reference. With a projection of his will, he changed his skin and hair to the same tones as hers—pale brown and black. He willed his horns away too, though it made him feel oddly naked. He tried to make himself smaller, but nothing happened. He'd reached the limits of the spell, apparently.

"Your eyes," Raiya reminded him.

He looked into her own eyes, studying the way her pupils darted with each shift in her attention. He gave himself her eyes—white with deep, dark centers ringed in a shining umber that reminded him of a pretty geode he'd once found.

She gave him her blanket to drape around his shoulders like a mantle, too, because apparently mortals considered it strange to leave one's torso uncovered.

***

IF SOMEONE HAD ASKED Azreth yesterday whether he could ever pass for something even vaguely resembling a human man, he would have scoffed.

The first time they crossed someone on the road after he'd donned his disguise, he was certain they would be caught, but the traveler just gave him an odd look as they went by.

Raiya was taking him to a human city called Ontag-ul, where she said she might find information on how to remove the binding runes on his hand. It was, unfortunately, several days away on foot. He could have flown them there faster, but summoning wings drained him, and it would draw unwanted attention.

Whenever he wasn't anxiously scanning the plains for danger, he was anxiously watching the mortal woman. She often shivered, pulling her cloak closer around herself. The yellow sun was bright here, but the air was as clear and cool as the water that filled the rivers and ponds. The cold was unforgiving. How long could mortals go without seeking refuge indoors? Would she grow ill if he kept her outdoors too long?

"Are you well?" he asked once after watching her put her hands to her red cheeks to try to warm them.

Her lips tilted into a smirk. "I'm well and strong. Don't think of betraying me. I will destroy you."

He sensed she was mocking him again, but he couldn't be certain, and he didn't want to make a fool of himself by asking her.

It was not long before he began catching glimpses of movement in the hills around them. Raiya did not seem to notice.

"We are being followed," he told her.

He half expected her to explain that this was a normal feature of her land, and that perhaps it was usual for other humans to follow each other like this, because she always seemed to have an explanation for everything. But when he spoke, she looked alarmed.

He moved closer to her, scanning the hills to count the approaching figures. If it was her husband coming to get her, he would protect her as he'd promised.

But Azreth didn't see Nirlan among them as the figures came closer. It was a group of humans riding on large, four-legged beasts with antlers, which shocked him. The kin never had such close contact with animals unless they were fighting. But these antlered creatures and the humans appeared friendly with each other.

There were half a dozen of them approaching, towering on their mounts. They wore bright silver armor, and hanging from their belts were swords, daggers, and quivers of arrows.

"Paladins," Raiya told him. "Followers of the god of justice, Paladius. They hunt demons, among other things."

He'd heard of them. Many of the mortal slaves in the hells had once been itinerant knights of their god Paladius. They wandered the planes searching for monsters to kill or mortals to rescue.

But here, the Paladins were in familiar territory. He suspected they would prove more formidable than they did in the hells.

"I know what they are," he said. He touched her arm, pulling her to a stop.

She peered up at him, suspicious. "What are you going to do?"

He just arched an eyebrow at her, because he assumed it was obvious. This was different from the farmhouse. These Paladins were armed and clearly had ill intent. How did she expect him to defend her and leave their enemies unharmed at the same time?

"Azreth, don't do anything rash. Paladins fight for good. They help people." She winced slightly, then added, "Supposedly. They are capable of seeing reason. If we can convince them you don't mean anyone harm, they won't hurt you. Maybe they could even help us. Don't do anything until I say so."

He bristled. "You do not command me." A part of him wondered if she would betray him to them. It was possible that allying with a demon hadn't been all she'd hoped for. Maybe these Paladins were better equipped to help her.

She quickly amended the order, grasping his arm gently. The touch sent a nervous prickle over his skin. "I'm asking you. As a favor. Please don't hurt anyone."

She was desperate again, like she'd been with the family in the farmhouse, her eyes wide and shining. It was an expression he'd only seen on her face when she was worried for someone else. Mortals cared for each other in a way kin didn't. Or at least, Raiya did.

Something twisted in his chest. When she begged him like this, like it was something important to her and he was the only one who could help, he felt an alarming desire to obey her.

He had to think rationally: she understood this land, and he didn't. He should accept her guidance. He wasn't foolish enough to make the same mistake twice.

So he turned to face the Paladins, his arms at his sides in a nonthreatening posture.

That lasted about two minutes.

To be fair to Raiya, she could not have known that these particular Paladins had been bought and sent by Lord Hangal, and were not simply a wandering patrol.

She was in the middle of trying to negotiate with them when Azreth spotted movement out of the corner of his eye. He looked up just in time to see an archer in the distance and an arrow already in flight.

He spun, pushing Raiya down and stepping in front of her. She made a startled sound as he caught the arrow in midair just before it hit him. A rank, metallic scent hit his nose, and he scowled, looking down at the arrowhead. Iron, of course.

One of the Paladins urged his mount forward and sped toward Azreth, his sword swinging low. Azreth sidestepped him, grabbing the man by his gauntlet and yanking him off his mount. He took hold of the collar of the man's cuirass with one hand, grabbed the base of the cuirass with the other, and smoothly used the momentum of the fall to fling the man twenty strides down the road. The sword nicked him in the process. He winced, looking down at the angry, dark slice in his forearm. Iron again.

He let his glamour fade. The mortals balked at the sight of him, even though they'd already guessed what he was, but they recovered composure quickly. They surrounded him, but they only attacked him from behind, so he was constantly spinning to fend off attacks. It was still not much of a fight. He evaded their iron weapons and took them down one at a time, knocking out some with his fists and kicking or throwing others.

After the blows stopped coming, he looked for Raiya and spotted her on the side of the road. He drew in a sharp breath. She was prone in the dirt, and a Paladin was on top of her, his arm locked around her neck, strangling her. Her skinny fingers clawed at his arm without effect, and the Paladin kept squeezing. The armored man was so much bigger than she was. How much pressure could her body take? How long could she go without air? Did he know he might kill her?

Of course he did. He had chosen to attack Raiya instead of Azreth because she was the smaller opponent. He had jumped at the chance to hurt someone who wouldn't be able to stop him.

Azreth's vision tunneled. He crossed the road rapidly, and the man looked up in surprise. He started to scramble up, reaching for his sword. Raiya gasped, sagging to the ground.

Azreth grabbed the Paladin and lifted him off his feet before he could move. It was as easy for him to kill the Paladin as it had been for the Paladin to attack Raiya. It was fitting, he thought, as he crushed the Paladin's chest and back between his palms. The man wheezed as his ribs snapped and caved in. The rich smell of fresh blood filled the air.

As Azreth dropped the Paladin's mangled corpse, Raiya stared up at him in horror, touching her throat. Her cheeks were speckled with red blood—not her own.

He paused for the first time since the fight had started, watching her face. Was she hurt? He began to reach for her, but she recoiled. Something inside him withered.

Setting his jaw, he turned to scan the road. There was only one Paladin left. The one Raiya had tried to negotiate with— he'd heard the man call himself Adamus—was standing a little farther down the road, watching them nervously.

When Azreth started toward him, Adamus quickly dropped his sword and held up his hands in surrender, which surprised him. But these Paladins were clearly not above deception—not that he could blame them, but it made them difficult to trust.

Azreth took him by the collar and picked him up off the ground. The Paladin made a short, choked noise before putting on a mask of calm. His face was unlined and slightly rounded with youth. His skin was pale and his hair was a light yellow-brown, anemic-looking, and Azreth wondered if he was unhealthy or if this was just his natural color.

The man closed his eyes and began reciting something under his breath. He was speaking to his deity. Or, trying to. *"Lord Paladius, I thank you for allowing me the honor of dying in your service. I return my body happily to Mother Astra, knowing I have done your will in fighting evil..."*

He didn't *sound* happy. Did mortals lie to their gods as much as they lied to each other?

Azreth could hear Raiya getting up and running to him, probably meaning to stop him from killing the Paladin. He exhaled softly in frustration.

He didn't like how he'd felt when she'd looked at him with fear and disgust. He didn't want her to look at him that way again. So instead of killing Adamus, he looked to Raiya, waiting for her to decide what they should do with him.

The Paladin proceeded to give several verbose but meaningless apologies, and then after very little discussion, Raiya sent him on his way, unharmed. Azreth couldn't believe it.

"Is this normal on your plane, to simply release enemies just because they ask for it?" he asked flatly, watching Paladin Adamus disappear down the road.

Raiya shrugged one shoulder. "Sometimes, if they've surrendered. It's considered dishonorable to execute someone after they throw down their weapons. There are certain rules for conflict."

"Rules? Who makes the rules?"

"No one, I suppose. It's about honor, like I said."

He understood that word, *honor*, but it was a mortal concept. In the hells, there was only individual survival by whatever means necessary. His people weren't tied to each other by a shared sense of duty and pride.

If those Paladins had really been honorable, they wouldn't have attacked Raiya, and they wouldn't have sent a sharp-shooter to try to kill him. They wouldn't have attacked without provocation.

It was a silly concept. It seemed designed to punish people who were truthful and merciful, and reward those who weren't.

Raiya was looking at him, as if trying to guess what he was thinking. Did she consider herself honorable? Did she think that he was not?

"I suppose it's different in the hells," she said finally. She sounded sad.

"In the hells, no one would bother to ask for mercy, because no one would ever grant it."

There was a soft sound—hooves scuffing the ground. The Paladins had left behind their animals, and now they stood alert in the grass on the edge of the road. They were very still, their heads raised as they watched him.

They were tall and cervine, long antlers topping long heads perched on long necks. The antlers made him wary. But their white fur looked like it would be soft and pleasant to touch. Instead of running or attacking, they waited, as if they still expected riders.

They were so calm. He'd never seen such tame animals before.

Something about them drew him in. He approached the closest one slowly, hand raised to touch it. But as soon as he came near, it scrambled away, kicking up a cloud of dirt. The entire group started, edging a little farther down the road. Azreth lowered his hand, frowning. He could have caught it if he'd chased it—but that wouldn't have been the same, would it?

Raiya came to stand beside him, tilting her head at him. "Do you... like animals?"

Did he?

Do you like...? It was such a mortal question.

What did he like? He liked things that didn't kill him, and things that fed him. Was there more to it than that? What else mattered?

He thought about how he'd imagined it would feel to touch the animal's fur. He'd hoped it was soft. He'd hoped the creature would look at him calmly, as if they were allies. He liked the idea of those things. Maybe he did like animals, then, when they weren't trying to devour him. Maybe he just liked soft things.

He thought of the softness of Raiya's hair when stray locks had brushed against him. He thought about the warm weight of her in his lap.

There was a scrape and a smear of dirt on her cheek where someone had shoved her face into the ground, but she smiled at him, still in good spirits.

He avoided her question. "Are they in danger here without their riders? Will something kill them if they're left alone?"

"Possibly." She gave them a thoughtful look, then looked up at him, perceptive. "You want to protect them." From someone in the hells, it would have been an accusation, but from her, it sounded like praise.

"Yes," he admitted.

"Why?"

There was no rational reason for it. He didn't have a good excuse to give her. "They're peaceful."

She just nodded in agreement. "We'll take care of them."

Raiya went to gather the animals. She approached them calmly, slowing when they shied away, and when she raised her hand to stroke their faces, they didn't run. Azreth felt a pang of envy.

They allowed her to pick up their tethers and lead them.

Soon, she had all of them following behind her, and she came back to where Azreth waited.

"Thank you," she said, surprising him. "For defending me."

If he had upset her before, she didn't hold a grudge. And for some reason, that made him feel relieved. "We have an alliance," he said.

TWELVE

The Roamer camp they encountered that evening was a nightmare.

Raiya explained that the Roamers were a clan of nomadic shepherds who lived in the northern parts of her country, Uulantaava. They lived in tents which they picked up and moved frequently, and they kept the same antlered creatures the Paladins had ridden—behelgi, Raiya called them. She said that running into the Roamers was fortuitous, because she could sell the Paladins' behelgi to them, and Azreth supposed that he was glad to have found a place where the animals would be protected from predators, but if it had been up to him, he still would never have risked entering this camp.

He'd had no idea it was possible for so many people to gather in one spot. There were dozens of them. People banged on drums and made other loud, repetitive sounds with screeching instruments. Younger mortals screamed and laughed and cried and chased each other (Raiya told him they were playing). Others were cooking and eating, fighting each other with wooden swords (practicing, Raiya said), rolling tiny squares of bone across the ground (a game, apparently) or moving their bodies in synchronized patterns in time with the drums (dancing). Before he could make sense of what one person was doing, his attention would be drawn to another, and another.

It was more noise and movement than he could keep track of. He couldn't possibly guard them from every sound in every direction. There was simply too much. As Raiya moved through the camp in front of him, his mind began to shut down. He fixed his eyes on her back, wishing he could turn off his senses.

Raiya was so completely relaxed that he supposed there truly must have been no danger, but he didn't know how she could look so comfortable in a place so chaotic.

He felt oddly small and foolish as he followed her through the camp. He'd been feeling that way often, lately.

The Roamers brought them to a fire, then gave them food and water. A young, blue-skinned elf girl named Jai sat beside them and cheerfully asked them many questions, which Azreth dodged. He listened absently while she and Raiya talked for what seemed like a very long time, discussing unimportant things like their home cities or their favorite foods. Talking was a form of entertainment to mortals, he realized. They did it for fun.

While Raiya spoke, he watched her. The longer she talked with Jai, the more she smiled, as if the girl's cheer was contagious.

He liked Raiya's smile.

He'd never been able to study someone this way, up close. There had been people like Nariel whom he had formed partnerships with, but he had never stared at them like this, never noticed the crinkles around their eyes and mouths when they smiled. Raiya's eyes squinted shut when she laughed hard enough, and when she grinned, he saw that her teeth were all flat; she had no fangs. He caught glimpses of her tongue. It was small and pink.

She grew happy and relaxed as they sat there, in the middle of this frenetic camp, talking to this stranger. When she wasn't looking, he adjusted himself so he was sitting slightly closer, so he could bask in her peace. The emotion wasn't quite strong enough to feed from, but it was pleasant, like bathing in a hot stream.

He had heard that mortals spent most of their lives in communities, forming close friendships and families, building societies and cities together. He saw now that what he'd heard was true. The fourth hell had cities, but not like this. Mortals were important to each other. Their relationships were important. He understood now why Raiya had suggested an equal partnership between them, because as he looked around, he didn't see anyone giving orders, nor anyone being beaten or taken advantage of. They saw others as equals by default.

Raiya greeted strangers as if she'd known them from birth, as if she trusted them implicitly and was pleased to see them. Companionship and happiness seemed to come so easily to her. Yes, she was often sad, but joy was always close by, within reach.

He felt a vague unhappiness now as he looked at her, though it took him a while to realize it.

Eventually, the elf girl left, and Raiya turned to Azreth. It was incredible how quickly her smile faded once she looked at him.

He was not like the mortals. She didn't feel a kinship with him the way she did with the others.

She looked him up and down, eyes narrow. "Are you all right?" she asked, but she wasn't really inquiring about his health. She expected him to turn on her at any moment. To her, he was an unpredictable, dangerous beast. He was an interloper here. His presence disrupted their peace.

He resisted the urge to snap at her. He didn't know what to say anyway, just that he felt like shouting at someone.

There was a man he'd been watching from across the camp. The man had only one leg. His trousers were rolled up on that side, pinned closed just below his hip, and he had no magical replacement limb like Azreth did. Several times now, Azreth had seen people bring him a plate or a cup or another item so that he didn't have to get up to fetch it himself. Even now, someone was bringing him crutches and helping him to his feet, and he was trembling as he tried to find his balance. Even if he hadn't been lame, he would have been frail and pitiful. Azreth scowled, nodding in his direction. "Why have they not just killed that one yet?"

Raiya raised her eyebrows. "Who?"

"The feeble one," Azreth said, jerking his invisible horns toward the man again.

"Who would want to kill him?"

"Everyone," he growled, impatient.

"I don't understand."

"*Look* at him. He cannot fend for himself. He can hardly walk. He is a drain on the resources of the group. Why should they protect him? Why not leave him behind?"

She gave him an unimpressed look. "Do you actually want me to answer that, or is this really about something else? Because I don't think you're as stupid as you're pretending to be."

Azreth looked away from her, clenching his jaw. After a few moments, he found he was too frustrated to sit still, and he got up.

"I will return," he said tersely, and he walked away from the fire.

He kept walking until he was at the edge of the camp, then turned to look back down the path through a colorful array of tents. In the twilight, a bonfire at the center of the camp glowed brilliantly, surrounded by carefree people. They were dancing, stumbling from the influence of the intoxicants they drank, while someone banged on drums incessantly.

It was all so *hideously* cheerful.

He imagined taking a sword and swinging it in a wide arc around the bonfire, cutting down five of them at once, mid-dance. He could cast a wave of fire that would set all their pretty tents aflame. He could tear into them one by one, in front of each other. They'd all fall to their knees, sobbing and keening as he drank their blood. He might not be able to have their happiness, but he could make their lives as terrible as his was. Mortals could build peaceful societies, but demons could break them.

He could turn all their joy to misery in an instant, and they didn't even know it. They didn't care. They danced on, blissfully unaware. He hated them.

"Well met, sair!" came a loud, high voice behind him.

He turned, startled. An elf child was peering up at him with interest, his tiny hand lifted in greeting. There was no one with him; he was wandering alone, without protection, as if he had nothing to fear. He was smiling broadly for no reason that Azreth could see—it was simply an inner joy that mortals were born with. But the smile quickly turned to a look of unease.

All Azreth's violent energy drained. He felt tired.

He attempted to tame his glower into a kinder expression, but it didn't quite work. The boy sensed his wrongness, even through the glamour, and Azreth felt a small but potent fear sprouting from him. The child spun and sprinted back toward the warm glow of the bonfire. Azreth watched him go.

A snort in the distance caught his attention, and he realized the Roamers' herd of behelgi was grazing on the hill behind him. They'd been so quiet that he'd not noticed them. It was a stark contrast to the chaos of the camp.

Slowly, he sat down in the grass near them. A few paused to glance up at him with dark eyes, but then they went back to nibbling on the endless supply of grass. A few of them had lay down to doze. They were perfectly at ease.

He wished he could be more like them.

THIRTEEN

TEN YEARS AGO

He stepped through the veil, and suddenly, he was.

Light burned his eyes, and he flinched. His chest jolted, and air filled his lungs. It was his first time taking a breath, but instantly he knew he could never go without breathing again. He became aware of things inside him churning and moving, a biological automaton starting up. Nerves sparked to life. Tiny lightning pulses passed across his brain. His heart juddered, then began thudding in his chest. Blood filled his limbs, and his muscles tightened with new strength.

Harsh wind blew grains of sand that stung his skin and stuck in his hair—because he *had* skin and hair. Realizing that, he looked down at his body. His skin was smooth and vibrant blue and perfect. He held out his hands in front of him—except, there was only one. His right arm was bent oddly, and it tapered to an anticlimactic end just past his elbow. This gave him pause, and he looked back and forth, comparing them. But if this was how he'd been made, he supposed this was how he was meant to be.

The fourth plane of hell stretched out before him, a vast

wasteland with a clouded, scarlet sky. It seemed to go on forever, for he could not see its end. Lightning flashed far in the distance, and thunder groaned. Cliffs and canyons of striated rock carved vicious lines into the earth. Small bits of brush and skeletal trees clung to life. Most of them were already dried and dead, burned and blackened.

It was an ancient, timeless place. It was beautiful.

Tears dampened his cheeks. He was filled with joy, because he existed. All of this—the wind, the earth, the sky—it existed, and it was impossibly fantastic that the chaotic threads of the universe had, by chance, spiraled into the exact shapes required to produce all of this, and to produce him.

And finally, as his body finished coming into the world, he felt something else: the feeling that would become the center of his being for the rest of his life.

Hunger. He craved bloodshed.

He was on the flat top of a tall, stone pyramid with steep steps leading to the ground. Crumbling columns and arches formed an arcade around him, and when he looked behind him, he saw the veil he'd stepped out of—a smear of black nothingness hanging in the air.

He was not alone. A dozen others watched him, their eyes sharp. The closest to him was a towering woman with emerald skin, yellow eyes like flames, and impressive horns that curved high over her head. She wore a headdress of fanning shards of metal and leather, and wide bracelets and necklaces of gold. Gold armor, dotted with bits of green that matched her skin, covered her from her neck to her thighs, and black and gold paint marked her body. She looked like a queen. Like a goddess. Like an eldress.

He instinctively knew her, and knew that he loved her, because she had brought him through the veil. She was the magnificently powerful being who had chosen to give him life. He was in awe of her.

But unease crept into him as he looked at her. Her lip was curling in distaste.

"What is your name?" she asked, her voice as cold and clear as thunder.

He had to think about it, but then it came to him, as if he'd known it long ago but had forgotten. "Azreth."

"Kneel, Azreth."

He hesitated, looking around at the others. They were waiting.

He did as she asked, dropping to his knees. The eldress came to him and took his face in one hand, her grip making his jaw ache. "You are our slave. You exist to serve." She cast a disgusted glance toward his right arm. "Though even for that, you are inadequate."

Comprehension slowly dawned on him. He was a disappointment to her. Shame filled him.

"What can I do?" he asked.

The eldress looked even more disgusted. "You can submit. It is what you were made for." She motioned toward the others. "It is what they were all made for. However, they became useful after they sated my hunger. You will never be useful. You will always be ugly and weak. So you will submit to us, weak one, and then you will die."

Azreth's brand new heart raced. Until that moment, it had not occurred to him that he could die. He had been alive for less than a minute, but he already knew he very much wanted to stay that way.

"I don't want to die," he said.

Someone hit him in the back of the head, and he pitched forward. For a split second, his vision went black, and then he was on the ground. Someone was grabbing one of his horns, wrenching his head back. When he tried to jerk away, someone else took hold of his wrist.

He fought back, but he had only one hand to strike and

grasp with. Even if he'd had only one opponent, he would have lost this fight.

He understood what the eldress meant now. He was flawed. Weak.

The eldress waved a hand, and a long, wicked knife appeared in her palm, its obsidian blade black and shining. Magic curled around it, making the edge glow. Azreth looked up at the eldress, pleading with her silently.

She raised an eyebrow. "Will you not fight?" she asked quietly. There was no mercy in her. She would never be tempted into kindness.

A new emotion crept over him, prickling on his skin. He examined it, letting himself experience this new feeling in full.

It was anger. It was sharp and uncomfortable, but it was better than misery. It gave him strength. It was a sort of power, even while he was powerless. It was all he had left.

The eldress seemed to sense this change in him, and she looked satisfied.

Then she brought the knife down and sliced clean through the shoulder of his malformed arm.

The eldress tortured him first, then she let the others take turns doing as they liked to him. Azreth fought until he grew too tired to do so, and then he fought some more. Once, he managed to strike one of them in the mouth, making them bleed, which gave him grim satisfaction for a few brief moments before they beat him even harder.

A night and a day and another night passed. There were many ways to wring all varieties of misery out of a person, it turned out.

Eventually, having subjected him to every kind of pain and degradation they could think of, their assaults slowed. They began to leave, one by one. The eldress lounged on a stone throne at the center of the top of the pyramid, watching her creation shudder in pain. Azreth's once smooth, new skin was now lined with cuts and bruises and fresh scars from wounds that had been quickly, haphazardly healed so that more could be layered on top of them.

As the last of the other demons disappeared down the steps of the pyramid, and the darkening skies rumbled with a storm that had been growing closer all day, the eldress gracefully unfolded her body from her throne and walked toward him. She carried the obsidian knife in her hand. Now that they were finished with him, he guessed she would kill him, so that his ugliness would no longer offend their eyes.

He was too drained to stand and fight her. Magic sparked at his fingertips, but he couldn't form a spell. He had tried to copy the patterns he'd seen them use to conjure weapons or move things with just their minds, but the magic felt wild and slippery, and he didn't know how to make it obey him.

The eldress looked down at him, impassive. They were alone, and it was quiet.

Somehow, he still loved and revered her, even now, and he wished she didn't despise him. He hated himself for it. What a foolish, pathetic emotion love was.

He waited for her to raise the knife and end his short life. But then something passed over her eyes. The hard lines in her face almost softened.

"Go," she said.

A silence followed. Azreth hesitated, trying to make sense of the word. Daring, he asked, "Why?"

She lifted a large, emerald hand and pointed to the stairs. "Leave the city. Never return. If you return, you will die."

Azreth waited, wondering what kind of cruel trick this was. But she said nothing more.

She watched him as he struggled to stand. Someone had cut through the back of his ankle, and it was impossible to put weight on that leg, but he managed to stagger to his feet and move to the stairs. He paused there, wanting to look back at his creator again before he left her forever. But he resisted the urge, and he climbed down the stairs one slow step at a time.

When he reached the bottom of the stairs, he looked out at the desolate landscape before him. Crumbling buildings and abandoned streets circled the pyramid, and the storm had moved in, blackening the sky. Dark, winged creatures soared above him, as if searching for prey. Searching for *him*, he supposed. He was prey—or he would be, unless he did something about it.

He lifted his hand to gingerly touch the tattered remains of his shoulder. He thought of the weapons he'd seen the other demons conjure—knives and clubs of pure magic energy, and he imagined magic taking the form of a new body part instead of a weapon.

FOURTEEN

Azreth thought of the eldress as he fiddled with the bracelet on his wrist.

The behelgi on the edge of the camp snorted softly behind him as he willed his glamour to change. The illusion of human skin on his hands pulled away, leaving blue behind on both, even his summoned arm. He turned the hands over, then back again, studying them.

With another thought, he removed the runes on his palm, too. Then he smoothed away the various scars on his fingers.

He stared at his palms, frowning.

He had thought to give himself a moment of self-indulgence, to imagine that he was wholly himself, untainted by the marks other people had left on him. But the more he changed, the less this body felt like his. He was accustomed to his scars, and taking them away didn't make him feel whole—it only made him feel like someone else.

But it didn't make him like the scars any more, either. If he disliked both his real self and his illusory self, where did that leave him?

Footsteps swished through the grass, and he quickly brought back his human color.

It was Raiya approaching. She slowed as he looked up. "Azreth? What are you doing out here?" He had thought she would be impatient, but she mostly seemed concerned.

"Nothing," he replied. He didn't get up.

She came to sit beside him. She began to reach toward him, then paused. "May I touch you?"

Remembering the way he'd snarled at her the first time she'd touched him, he felt foolish. He hadn't realized how freely mortals touched each other. She'd only been doing what came naturally to her, and reacting so explosively had only revealed a vulnerability of his. "You don't need to ask."

She took his hand. Azreth waited, but she just sat with him, curling her fingers around his. He had seen a few of the other people in the camp holding hands this way as they sat or walked together, like they were reluctant to part with each other. He had thought it was a gesture of affection, but now that she was doing it to him, he wasn't sure.

"We're safe here, you know," she said. "You shouldn't be afraid."

"I'm not," he said evenly, staring toward the dimming bonfire.

Raiya said nothing, but tilted her head in front of him to force him to look at her. She searched his face, looking into one eye and then the other. The wind blew strands of her dark hair across her face, and he caught a hint of her scent—not her emotions, but her body.

"Be at ease," she said, and he realized she was repeating his own words back to him. And this time, her voice had no mocking tone. She thought he was in need of comfort.

She could have spent the evening with the other mortals, laughing and dancing like the rest of them. She could even have shared her body with one of the other human men here if she craved companionship. But instead, she was here, with him.

"The glamour makes you forget what I am," he commented.

"I have not forgotten," she assured him. "Would you rather I cringed away in fear?"

"No. Your passion pleases me more."

Her expression was guarded, but he saw her draw a slow breath. An invisible heat pulsed from her, a shiver in the air. She stood and tugged on his hand. "Come."

The more time he spent with her, the more he was beginning to feel like he was her prisoner, not the other way around.

THEY RETURNED to their tent for the night so that Raiya could feed him. As soon as the door to the tent was sealed, he let his glamour fade. Raiya watched him with an expression he couldn't quite read. Her emotions were muddled.

He wanted her, selfishly. He wanted to give her pleasure so that he could feel what she felt. He wanted to take her joy for himself, like the parasite he was.

He moved close to her. "May I begin?" he asked.

She put a hand to her face, and he heard her swallow nervously. "Yes. You'll have to give me a minute..."

He pulled back a little. That wasn't how he'd hoped she would react. "To do what?"

"To try to get in the mood. It's not that easy to do, sometimes."

He frowned. He had thought she might not be enthusiastic, but he hadn't thought she would have performance anxiety. "You do not need to do anything. I will take what I need from you, as you've requested." He brought his hand between her legs. The sooner he began, the sooner she would stop feeling this stress.

"I know, but—" She sucked in a surprised breath as he touched her, and her body went rigid, but she didn't move away.

He got the feeling, as his fingers homed in on her, that mortals didn't approach intercourse in such a straightforward way. But she didn't seem to dislike it. "You may relax. We've established that I can bring you to completion."

She started breathing again. He had worried she might have changed her mind about letting him touch her, but then she leaned into him slightly, resting her hands on his forearms. Warmth thrummed through his chest. He wasn't certain if it was her emotions he was feeling, or his own.

Feeling her arousal in the air, seeing the way she excited from his touch—it awoke a now-familiar desire in him. His body wanted hers for more than just feeding. He couldn't pretend it didn't.

"I enjoy touching you," he murmured, though he knew it was strange for him to appreciate a mortal this way. He expected her to react to that confession with disgust or fear, but the emotion he felt coming from her was more akin to interest.

"Do you?" she asked, looking up at him from beneath her lashes. Need pounded through him.

He put his arm around her, pulling her up against his chest, and he carried her to the floor and laid her on her back. The outline of her body was only faintly visible through her thick clothes, which she needed to protect herself from the cold. He'd never encountered people who wore as many clothes as the people in Uulantaava did.

It had the curious effect of making her even more enticing. He imagined peeling off her clothing piece by piece to reveal more of her skin, to see how she reacted when he touched it.

He leaned close to her, letting his lips brush the cloth over the crux of her thighs. He still wasn't sure what she would allow. He knew he could bring her to new heights of pleasure with his tongue, but he was certain it would frighten her. He'd seen the wary way she'd looked at his teeth.

"I will feel your skin now," he said. "I will slick my hand with what is gathering between your thighs before I make you come." He glanced up at her, uncertain. She looked surprised, but she nodded. Fire went through him.

"Remember the rules," she said quickly.

He was already pulling off her trousers and underclothes. "I have not forgotten." But he did forget himself a little as he roughly flipped her onto her hands and knees. He heard her gasp as he jerked her hips back against him.

His breath caught as the curve of her backside pressed into his thighs, his hardening cock nestling against her from behind his sarong. Instinctively, his hips locked and he thrust against her as his hands held her tightly in place.

This was too much. His attraction to her was unnatural. He'd never heard of someone behaving this way with a mortal. There was a difference between being fed and being seduced. He was meant to take joy in the weakness of mortals because of his power over them, not because he found beauty in their softness and gentleness.

It wasn't that he enjoyed this because she was his for the taking—he enjoyed it because she *allowed* him to take her. Her consent and trust were an unexpected, taboo thrill. He had never seen a mortal earnestly enjoy what a demon did to them. It hadn't occurred to him that it could be done this way.

They had both been forced into this arrangement out of desperation, but at that moment, there was only willing pleasure.

It was with no small amount of shame that he continued, unable to convince himself not to. He ran his hand over the soft, warm flesh of her hip, creased where her thighs bent. He could feel muscle beneath the surface, but it was cushioned by a layer of velvety skin. It was like she'd been made to be touched.

Absently, he summoned a third hand to run through her hair. It was slightly tangled from their time on the road, but it still felt as silken as it looked.

Raiya jerked, her fear spiking. She turned to look back at him accusingly, and then she saw his summoned hand.

It occurred to him that she'd never met his hands before, other than the one he used to replace his right arm. He directed the disembodied hand—the same transparent magenta as his arm, cut off at the wrist—to float in front of her where she could examine it. She looked surprised, but not displeased. So he made more of them.

The summoned hands touched her in all the places he couldn't reach, all the parts of her that he wanted his hands on while his flesh-and-blood fingers crept between her thighs. A shudder went through her. Her head bent toward the floor, her body pushing backwards against him. All the fear and reticence was gone, and only wanton need was left.

He imagined freeing his cock and sinking into her. The thought sent fire over his skin, and also repulsed him. For an instant, he was transported back to the hells. Strong, rough hands forced things into his mouth, wove disgusting spells into him, touched and stroked him until he was forced to take pleasure in violation.

Bile rose in his throat. He could not tolerate being touched. He had only been able to complete intercourse with Nariel because she used magic to keep him ready.

He focused on her body instead of his: The softness of her bare skin. The quiet gasps she made. The way her muscles tensed and released beneath his touch.

She was nothing like any of the demons he'd met. She was

content to let him give her pleasure without ever trying to take his. She didn't demand anything in return. She didn't push back. She didn't bite.

It was his own selfish desire, rather than desire to please her, that drove him to press a hand against her entrance until she allowed his finger to slip into her. She gasped, her hands clenching, and the inside of her body felt as hot and strong as molten metal. She began to choke out a word, but it became a whimper, and she leaned back, pushing him deeper.

Her climax washed over him, airy and thick and perfect. It sank into him through her sex, through every part of her that was touching him.

He closed his eyes and saw stars. It was beyond anything he'd ever felt with another person. It was so good that it frightened him, because surely something this good couldn't come without a cost.

A minute passed as she panted, her limbs trembling. Azreth took at least as long to recover, but he eventually released her, letting his summoned hands disappear.

And then... the sweet taste of her pleasure turned to ash in his mouth as another feeling quickly replaced it. She had suddenly become deeply unhappy. He watched her curl up on the floor of the tent, her face to the ground.

A jolt of fear went through him. Had he hurt her?

It shouldn't have mattered. He should have drunk down her sadness just as easily as her lust, the same way he'd devoured Eunaios's despair as he died. But he couldn't. Some meals always made him sick. Maybe he had some illness that prevented him from digesting them—a birth defect, like his arm.

There was something familiar about her melancholy. He realized he'd felt it before. It was the same muddled anger, sadness, and shame he always felt when intercourse was complete. He hadn't realized there were other people who felt that, too.

Was she recalling bad memories, like Azreth was?

After a time, she rose, sitting back on her knees, as if determined to pretend away her own regret, but she said nothing. Azreth knew how to make a mortal come, but he had no idea how to fix unhappiness. He thought of grabbing her and commanding her to stop feeling this bad feeling. That probably wouldn't help.

He wrapped his arm around her, seeking her warmth and softness, but he knew that his own body was harsh and heavy and could not offer her the same comfort in return.

"Be at ease, Raiya," he said helplessly.

To his surprise, she rested a hand on his arm, hugging him against herself. "I am," she said, but it was a lie.

Truthfully, nothing about any of this should have been surprising.

He was a demon, after all. He was made for breaking things.

FIFTEEN

It was not until they were on the road to Ontag-ul again that, after far too many days of abstaining, Azreth finally worked up the courage to sleep.

No, that wasn't accurate. He never really gained the courage—just the desperation. Even demons couldn't go without rest forever.

So many horrible things could be done to an unconscious person. He feared sleeping more than almost any other task in life. But he didn't fear Raiya. Or at least, he feared her less than he feared anyone else, mortal or demon. Was he a fool to feel that way?

He dreamed of brown eyes, tawny skin, and expressive black brows. In the dream, he felt happy. Had he ever felt happy before?

He couldn't recall the woman's name, but he knew they were companions, and he was glad she was with him. They were together on the ground in his cave in the fourth hell, resting in the warm, dark earth. She was smiling at him. Their hands touched. She rolled closer, leaning into him, entwining their bodies. He held her close, pressing his face close to hers.

And then, to his horror, he felt his teeth sinking into her flesh. He tried to stop, but his jaw would not unclench. He held her down and bit clean through her neck, ignoring her struggles. Her warm, fragrant blood burst from the wound, spilling over both of them. She was going to die.

He pulled back, agonized. Why had he done this? Why hadn't he just stopped?

And then, pain cut across his throat. Looking down, he found an iron dagger in the woman's hand. Each of them had secretly plotted against the other.

She raised the dagger and stabbed again and again with strength that only seemed to increase as she neared death. Her head was at a grotesque angle, mostly separated from her body, but her expression was cold and calculating. Pain came in bursts where the blade hit him. He didn't try to stop her.

Azreth awoke suddenly. The dark blue sky, dotted with stars and turning lavender on the horizon, stretched above him. Cool, watery air filled his lungs. His heart was pounding.

Raiya was sitting beside him, legs stretched out casually in front of her, her baton on her lap. She gave him an easy smile. "Good morning."

He stared at her dumbly, which seemed to amuse her.

"Do you feel better?" she asked, arching an eyebrow.

He glanced down at his hand, checking the runes. She would have had time to paint new ones on him while he slept, if she'd wanted. Maybe she could even have found a way to channel magic into them and activate them, to curse him in some new way that would serve her. But even before he looked, he'd known that nothing in his body had changed. No new magics had attached themselves to him, and no part of him was injured.

She hadn't touched him. She'd sat beside him, protecting him. And she casually said good morning, like it was nothing.

In retrospect, that may have been the moment when he'd begun to fall in love with her.

Raiya checked his hand, as she did each morning. She said she wanted to make sure the enchantment was not changing. He had begun to feel a strange, nervous anticipation for the examination each morning. He was not afraid, but his heart raced and his nerves lit up when she came toward him.

She held his hand in both of hers, her thumbs pressing down on the edges of his palm. He felt hyperaware of her touch: the temperature of her fingers, the texture of her skin, and the tiny movements of muscles and tendons in her hands. Her hands were cold from the early morning air, and her fingers were thin but dexterous and precise in their movements.

"It looks much the same," she said thoughtfully. "Unfortunate."

He watched the top of her head as she tilted his hand to let the faint runes catch the light. "Why is that unfortunate?"

She shrugged, releasing his hand. "I had hoped it might start to fade. The enchantment wasn't completed, after all, so it was possible it wouldn't hold. But it looks like the gods haven't favored us."

"Have the gods ever favored us?" he asked dryly.

She laughed. Another odd, nervous feeling went through him at the sound. "No, I think not."

He didn't realize until afterward that he'd called them *us.* He had never been part of an *us* before.

***

IT WAS night when they finally arrived in the city of Ontagul, and water was falling from the sky.

He first noticed it when something tapped against one of his horns. He reached up to brush it away, thinking it was an insect, and his hand came away wet. When he looked up, he realized there were tiny drops of liquid pelting the ground around him. He reached for Raiya's arm.

"It's rain," she said, having already guessed the reason for his alarm. "Another thing you don't have in the hells?"

He looked up, trying to find the origin of the water. The open, cloudy sky sprawled above them. "Is it a magical anomaly?" he asked, thinking of the bursts of dangerous, chaotic magic that occasionally appeared in the hells.

Raiya smiled. She never tired of his questions about her plane. She was what mortals called an academic: a person devoted to study. At first, he'd thought she would look down on him for his ignorance. But after a while, he'd realized that she seemed to like people who asked questions more than people who didn't. "No. It's a gift from Astra from when she created the world. We'd die without it."

"Then it's not dangerous?"

"Not if you don't get stuck in it for too long."

Ontag-ul was even more populated than the Roamer camp had been, but with more space, and more alcoves and pathways to take refuge in. It was darker and quieter, and he could go unnoticed more easily, observing its inhabitants from a safe distance. He liked it better here.

When he said as much, Raiya replied, "Or maybe you've just become accustomed to being around mortals. We don't frighten you anymore."

"I was never frightened," he said evenly.

"Perhaps you're just starting to like our plane, then."

"No."

She just hummed noncommittally.

He had to admit that he found the city fascinating. Their buildings were made of tree matter, bundled grasses, and clay tiles. Stone paths snaked through tight outdoor corridors lit by hanging lanterns and torches. It smelled wet and green and alive. Dark green trees and vines crowded around the buildings, as if the city had sprouted from a garden. Maybe it had? He had no idea how mortal cities came to be.

The place was filled with wild plants, colorful draping fabric and tooled leather, and stones with inlaid bits of metal. It reminded him of the Roamers' tents and carpets and clothing, all made with a huge variety of patterns of color and texture.

It all made him feel mildly frustrated in the same way the Roamer camp had frustrated him. "This city is not very defensible, aside from the wall," he commented.

"I think it's very pretty," Raiya replied.

"Pretty?"

She gestured around them. "The architecture. The plants. Do you have artists in the hells?"

The word floated in his mind, lacking form. He understood it, but not really. "What is an artist?"

Raiya's face pinched ever so slightly. She pitied him. She often looked at him like this, though she tried to hide it.

"It's a person who makes beautiful things for a living," she explained. She pointed to the intricate wooden lattice that covered the window of the building beside them. "These details serve no defensive purpose. They exist just to be beautiful. Because they're nice to look at, and they make you feel at home. Things like that are made by artists and artisans."

Azreth reached out and touched the latticework. He had crafted tools from wood and stone before, but nothing like this, which must have required such skill and time and imagination. It was a complex array of wood, lovingly shaped into organic patterns resembling flowers and leaves and animals, arranged so perfectly that it looked as if their goddess Astra might have made the wood grow that way.

Rain water was dripping through a crack in the roof, down the lattice, and a damp, green trail had grown there. The water would erode the wood and eventually it would decay into nothing, but it would still outlast the mortal who'd carved it. Perhaps that person was already gone.

Azreth looked at it for a long time. And he realized maybe Raiya was right to pity him.

Mortals didn't waste their lives fighting each other like the kin did. They spent their time creating instead of destroying, building things that were pretty and comfortable and thoughtful instead of merely strong. There was more to their lives than just survival.

He felt deep sorrow as he contemplated that. He felt a sense of loss.

"Demons don't think about the beauty of things." His voice sounded remote, even to himself.

"What about you?" Raiya asked. "Do you think about beauty?"

He looked down at her. One of her smooth, dark, beautiful brows was arched at him. Knowing. Almost accusing. Waiting for him to acknowledge what was obvious.

He supposed he did think about beauty sometimes, after all.

JUST WHEN HE'D started to fear he liked this city, they entered an inn.

It was busy and loud and filled with people carrying weapons and people who eyed them too long—or, in the case of the owner, insulted them to their faces. He was relieved when Raiya told him to wait in their rented room while she went to retrieve food.

But once she left, he began thinking of all the people crowding the main room of the inn. People with weapons.

Men who had looked at him with envy. Men who had made her shrink with worry.

He sat on the bed and waited a short while, and then he got to his feet again, glamouring himself as he went out the door.

He half expected to run into her on the other side of the door, but the hallway was empty. Nor was she in the main room of the inn.

She would say he was overreacting, and that there was no danger. There was rarely danger in the mortal world, it seemed. Mortals were mostly kind to each other. She had probably just gone outside, and any moment now she would come back in and laugh at him for worrying.

But then he imagined someone dragging her away while she struggled. He recalled Nirlan shoving her into his cage, and the Paladin who'd nearly crushed the life out of her.

He weaved through the crowded room and exited onto the dark street.

He stood very still, listening. A stream of rainwater flowed from the corner of the eaves and pattered against the muddy ground. People chattered as they darted along the street, pulling hoods over their heads to keep out the rain. Everything was calm.

Then he heard a burst of something magical in the distance. Over the tops of the tiled roofs across the street, there was a faint flash of blue light.

Raiya's baton.

His heart sped to a buzz. Raising his hands, he gathered magic.

Sparkling fractals of magic energy crackled at his fingertips as he wove them into a spell. He felt magic tingling at his scapulae, and then the magic solidified into the shape of draconic wings made of magenta light.

The people on the street stopped and stared. Azreth

stretched the wings, adjusting to the unfamiliar sensation of straining muscles in his back and the resistance of air beneath him, and then he launched into the sky.

He almost fell from the air on the second flap of the wings. It had been months since he'd used them. Demons of the fourth hell were not born with wings. He'd first summoned them as an experiment based on the spell he'd designed to replace his arm, and he'd had to learn to fly on his own. But it was by far the fastest way for him to get from one place to another.

It didn't take him long to regain his balance. He rose above the buildings, then landed on a rooftop where he could see more of the city. His gaze was drawn to a tangle of movement on the next street. A group of men in Paladin's armor were jostling below.

A shock went through him when he spotted Raiya—though he barely recognized her. The Paladins were holding her while she struggled. Her face was a mess of angry tears. He was too far away to feel her emotions, but somehow he felt them anyway, and her rage became his own.

He dove from the rooftop.

They saw him coming just before he landed. The Paladin he was aiming for looked up, and Azreth crashed into him, pinning him to the ground before putting a fist through his chest. He resisted the urge to punch him again and again—the man was already dead.

He spun toward Raiya. The Paladin who'd been holding her was backing away, drawing an iron sword. Azreth strode forward and grabbed him by the arm. There was a click as the man's arm dislocated from his shoulder, and he flew like a rag doll when Azreth threw him across the road.

Rapid footsteps hit the muddy ground behind him, and he twisted to avoid the end of an iron-tipped spear. At the same time, he heard the snap of a bowstring releasing.

The spear wielder's momentum carried him in front of Azreth, and Azreth picked him up by the back of his cuirass. With a flap of his wings to pull him out of the path of the archer's arrow, he hurled the spear wielder across the street, into the archer. Both of them hit the ground in a metallic heap.

Bystanders screamed and ran. The remaining Paladins retreated with them.

Azreth turned to Raiya, breathless. He scanned her, head to toe, checking for injuries, and saw none. Her face softened as she looked at him, rain mixing with the tear tracks on her face. As everyone else ran from him, she started toward him.

Azreth began to go to her, then stopped. He sensed the human lord before he saw him, somehow—not through any magical means, but some other unconscious animal awareness. He'd only ever seen one person make Raiya this furious and sad before; maybe that was how he knew.

When he turned around, he found Nirlan Han-gal standing a dozen steps behind him.

Azreth stiffened. A strange sense of dread filled him, rooting his feet to the ground. For a moment, he was back in his cage in the castle's dungeon; trapped, chained, starving, bound.

He shouldn't have felt fear, but he did. He wanted to flee. It was absurd. Shameful. He was a demon. This was a mortal, a mere man. A man he despised, who had hurt himself and Raiya both. There was no magical barrier between them now. He could destroy him with a single strike.

Hunger for violence still pounded through his body. He suspected it was that hunger, more than courage, that drove him to move toward Nirlan.

The man went pale as he approached. The scent of his fear was heavy, caressing Azreth like bloodied velvet. His death would be delicious.

Nirlan drew a knife and swung it in front of him, but it was mere steel. Azreth didn't even bother to block the attack. The blade scratched against his skin, denting the metal. As Nirlan waved the knife ineffectually, he slipped in the mud and fell, nearly stabbing himself in the process.

He was a ridiculous, pathetic man. And yet he possessed an enormous castle, a perfect wife, and a bevy of armed servants and mages to do his bidding. It appeared that you didn't have to be strong or clever or skilled to succeed in the mortal realm. Maybe you only needed to be cutthroat.

"Raiya! Help me!" Nirlan demanded. Without his servants, he had no power, no will to fight, no strength.

Azreth looked over at Raiya, and he was pleased to see her looking at Nirlan with as much disgust as himself.

"For the love of Astra, call him off!" Nirlan cried. Raiya gave him a look that was pure hatred. Azreth could feel it radiating from her. It was a beautiful feeling.

She looked at Azreth and nodded her approval, her eyes grim and furious. Azreth could still faintly see the redness in her eyes from when she'd cried.

He reached toward Nirlan's throat, and he was trying to decide whether it would be more agonizing to be strangled to death or to bleed out slowly, when his vision suddenly shattered.

A thread of pain between his hand and his neck lit up, blinding, propelling him backward. For a moment, the world was gone, and only agony existed.

When his vision returned, he was kneeling on the ground, rain rippling the puddles around him. It smelled of blood and earth. Raiya was speaking. He could feel her hand on his arm.

Azreth swayed, stunned. The moment he'd touched Nirlan, he'd been repelled. His neck felt like it had been cut, though the skin was unbroken, and his palm burned like it had been struck with iron. When he lifted his hand, he was startled to see the runes glowing and steaming like a fresh brand.

The half-binding had protected Nirlan. It had burned Azreth in the same place he'd tried to grab him, reflecting the injury back before he could do any damage.

Azreth was nauseated. He couldn't hurt Nirlan. These cursed runes were a shackle on him, and he was trapped in his own enchanted body.

Yet again, Nirlan—this mere mortal—had defeated him.

Raiya's hand tightened on his cloak. "Azreth." When he looked up, Nirlan was coming toward them, an iron sword in his hand.

Azreth pulled Raiya against his chest, then flapped his wings and leapt into the air. They shot above the street, above the buildings, into the sky.

Raiya's arms clamped around his neck. Her face was buried in the crook of his shoulder, her breath hot against him. He clutched her a little tighter. Below, the Paladins were regrouping with Nirlan, and they were chasing him.

Azreth didn't know where to go next. He was lightheaded, and each flap of his wings was difficult. Summoning the wings in the first place had drained him more than he'd anticipated, and whatever Nirlan's enchantment had done to him had drained him further.

He flew to a tall building at the edge of the town. A slender tower rose from one side of it, and he landed in its shadow on the tiled roof, swooning a little. He carefully set Raiya on her feet beside him. She held onto him, probably just trying not to slip off the sloping roof, but he could pretend it was because she needed his touch.

Then he smelled blood. He looked down sharply. Her hand was bleeding. She must have been hit with a blade during the fighting.

Without thinking, he lifted her wound to his mouth to

clean the blood away, and he didn't even know why he would do such a thing—an instinct left over from a more primitive era? It was certainly not out of hunger or violent urges toward her—but it felt like the right thing to do, until he saw her face. She looked at him with vague confusion, her mouth slightly ajar. He stopped, wondering if she'd be upset, like when he'd tried to snake his hand beneath her trousers.

But she did not look offended. She didn't move away from him. In fact, she stayed very close, holding onto him.

"Thank you," she said. "Again."

He stared at her, loving the way she looked at him.

He felt something, then. A deep, unfulfilled desire taking root deep within him. Something like... longing.

A frisson of fear went through him.

He took a step back, snapped out of whatever madness had begun to take him. He should not have had these feelings. He should not have worried for her. He should not have been thinking of her as someone to be held and cared for, or as someone who would hold and protect him in return. She was his ally—which merely meant that she was temporarily not his enemy. They were not companions. Demons did not have companions.

Raiya just looked at him. Her hand was still bleeding, and she was shivering. The rain had made the cold sink into her.

He healed the cut on her hand with a spell, which drained the last of his magic. His wings and his arm both disappeared, and he staggered. When Raiya put her small hands around his shoulders in a vain but valiant attempt to steady him, he felt another stab of something powerful and dangerous in his heart.

He would not say the word—not even to himself, in his mind. He couldn't think it, couldn't make it real.

"Are you all right?" Raiya asked.

"I am still strong," he said faintly.

The Paladins were racing around the streets below, searching for them. They'd spot him eventually. And they were stuck on the roof with no way down. He hadn't thought this through.

"Hello there!" someone said in a harsh whisper, very close.

He spun to face the voice. An old woman was peering out from an open window on the roof that he hadn't seen before. Her face was white as sun-bleached bones, but the color was smeared around the edges of her hair, like she'd painted it on. Black paint circled her eyes, and she was smiling, which made her face resemble a skull.

"The lady of darkness welcomes you," she said. "You are being pursued by the Paladins, yes? Come inside the temple. Hurry."

Azreth glanced at Raiya for an explanation. Looking at her expression, he couldn't tell whether she felt comforted or threatened by this woman.

"Moratha cultists. Like Eunaios," Raiya told him under her breath.

Eunaios—the mage who'd kept him caged in Nirlan's dungeon. Azreth was suddenly imagining burning the temple down.

Raiya gave him a sympathetic smile. She took his hand. "Come on."

He folded his fingers around hers. Against his better judgment, he let her pull him toward the window.

SIXTEEN

The old woman, Gereg, was a sort of eldress that mortals called a priestess. She believed that Azreth had been sent by their goddess to fulfill some kind of vague death prophecy. Moratha was the mortals' goddess of death, and to mortals, demons were bringers of death, so he supposed he couldn't fault their reasoning.

She showed them around the temple while she told them all this. Everywhere they went, stares followed. The cultists did not seem afraid of him. That made him nervous.

He walked among them unglamoured, and instead of running in terror, they followed him around and fawned over him, bowing low and staring in awe and showering praise. Perhaps someone with more sense or patience would have found a way to take advantage of this, but he just wanted them gone.

Unfortunately, he needed them. They had mages, books, and supplies that might help Raiya craft a counter-enchantment to remove his binding. And the Paladins couldn't enter the temple while the cultists were guarding them. So when they discussed apocalyptic prophecies and waxed poetic about their own mortality, Raiya just nodded blandly.

"Your companion doesn't speak much, Acolyte Raiya," Gereg said after a while, studying Azreth with a keen eye. Azreth just frowned at her, because he didn't know what to say, and because he already didn't like her.

Raiya gave that easy, charming smile of hers, and said without missing a beat, "He is still new to the mortal plane. Our customs are unfamiliar to him, so he prefers to let me speak for him."

He could tell that Raiya believed herself to be telling a lie. Maybe she thought she had pressured him into allowing her to speak for him. Maybe she didn't know how relieved he was to have an intermediary between himself and the other mortals. If she hadn't been with him, his life would have reverted to violence and chaos long ago.

She always knew what to say to ease tensions and build friendships. She was good at that. It had worked on him, after all. Azreth didn't know how to talk to mortals. He didn't even know how to talk to other kin. It was easier to just keep his distance from others.

After what felt like hours, the priestess finally left them alone in the temple's main hall.

Azreth turned to Raiya. He hadn't fully appreciated how much he liked being alone with her until the cultists had begun crowding around. Even now, a few of them hovered on the edges of the room, staring.

Raiya noticed him looking at her, and she smiled tiredly, like they were sharing a secret.

He needed to feed. He did not want to ask, but he had completely run out of magic. He'd had to dispel his false arm, which he never did if he had a choice. He had long ago come to terms with his missing limb, but it was still a weakness, and he disliked being reminded of it. Having his deformity on display for all to see shamed him.

He imagined Raiya would grow tired of being put in this position. She must have already suspected he would do nothing to her if she refused him. He could only ask her, and hope her generosity didn't run out.

He touched her back, indulgently running his fingers up to her exposed neck above her cloak. Her skin was damp and cold.

"I am hungry," he said, regretful.

To his surprise, her dark eyes got darker. "So am I." Her smile had quirked up on one side, giving it a sultry edge. She met his gaze and didn't look away, though her cheeks had grown redder. She was blushing.

Heat gripped him, burning in his chest—a pleasant pain, which was worrying. Pain should never feel pleasant.

She cleared her throat, looking away. "Later," she promised.

He nodded, mute.

THE MOMENT RAIYA left his side, cultists rapidly closed in. They caught him in a hallway, blocking his path forward. He didn't think they meant him harm, but it made him nervous to be so close to so many people, and he suppressed the instinct to beat his way through them.

"Great Servant of Moratha!" said one of them in greeting, bowing low. The others bowed in unison, too. "We are most honored by your presence. The High Priestess tells us a great awakening is coming."

It was absolutely bizarre seeing mortals so happy to see him. "...Yes," he said.

The cultist smiled wide. "We are your humble servants. What would you have us do?"

"Help my companion find a way to break the curse on me."

The cultist dipped his head. "Of course. And after that, Dark One? What does the dark lady wish of us?"

Azreth just stared at him. He had no idea what their goddess wanted, but he couldn't very well say so.

The cultist took his silence in stride. "Do you require blood sacrifices?"

Against his better judgment, he paused to consider that. It sounded like something he'd like. "Sacrifices?"

"Yes!" The man drew a knife from within his robes and ushered two young female cultists forward to kneel in front of him. "They're virgins, of course. Or would you prefer the blood of a child? Or a priest of Astra, perhaps?"

Azreth did not completely understand what a virgin was, but he gleaned it was something to do with sex.

He considered the group for a moment. The girls in front of him were stiff, and their eyes darted, avoiding him.

The offer was not tempting.

His life had become so strange. Mortals were throwing themselves at him now, and he didn't even want them.

"At your word, my lord." The male cultist raised his knife to the throat of one of the girls in front of him, and Azreth suddenly understood that this "blood sacrifice" involved killing, not merely bleeding. The man was grinning excitedly, but the girl's fear was filling the hall.

Azreth contemplated demanding the man's own life instead, just to see if he'd retract his offer. But he wasn't confident the man wouldn't joyfully slit his own throat, and Raiya probably wouldn't like it if she found out he'd made a man kill himself.

"Why would I want that?" Azreth asked, not bothering to hide his annoyance. "What good does it do me?"

The cultist looked startled. He quickly recovered, sheathing the knife. The girls were visibly relieved.

"They would be honored to serve you in other ways, too, of course," the man said. "We have many beautiful maidens among us. And if none here take your fancy, we will procure others. Whatever you wish. The town is full of delights of the flesh."

"No," he replied simply. The cultist blinked at him. They were all still blocking the hallway in front of him. Azreth was so impatient to get away from them that he just turned and walked the other way.

"Very well, my lord!" the cultist called after him. "We are at your service, my lord! Whenever you wish to begin, we will be ready!"

AZRETH STOOD beside Raiya's bed in the sleeping quarters that night to guard her sleep. At least, he tried to, but after an hour of cultists sidling up to him to ask for favors or whisper their desires for servitude, Raiya became annoyed and told him to wait outside.

The night became a tiring game of avoiding the cultists, many of whom seemingly didn't sleep. Their temple was pleasantly dark and quiet, and it was easy to find secluded spots, but somehow they always found him. He would never admit it aloud, but on one occasion he glamoured himself completely brown-black to blend in with the wall of a dark room and avoid notice.

In the morning, he went to the sleeping quarters to wake Raiya, and her bed was already empty and tidy, as if she'd never been there. He found her some time later in a room that was filled to the brim with hundreds, maybe thousands, of books on shelves. It should have been the first place he looked for her.

She was sitting on her knees, bent over a large, old-looking book. Her hair draped beside her face. Her hands were splayed on either side of the book, her brow slightly furrowed as she read. She looked nice like this. He didn't know why. She was always pretty, but even more so right then, somehow.

He knelt beside her, but she didn't notice him, and he didn't interrupt her work to greet her. He watched her read until she happened to sit back and look up. She smiled when she saw him. A flame in his heart lit up, burning him.

She was the only one in this temple who really wanted him, and not just to use him. It shouldn't have mattered, but it did. He liked being wanted.

It was a very mortal way of thinking. Raiya's ways were rubbing off on him, and that probably should have worried him.

"Look what I found," she said excitedly, pointing at the old book. "It was written by an Ysuran mage who lived in the fourth century. It's a study of runes found on enchanted arti-facts from the hells. Look at these. They're very similar to the ones on your hand." She flipped through pages, pointing as she went. "And here—this section has theories about reversing bindings. Most of it isn't relevant to you, but look at this set of runes. The runes on your hand appear to be a combination of several languages and spell types, but I think some of them use an old demonic language. We can use this as a basis for building a spell to reverse your binding. I've already made a few prototype enchantments for us to test."

Azreth stared at the book, then at her notebook, dazed. Prototypes. Spells.

He asked slowly, "You can read all these runes? These spells?"

"Yes, most of them. I've studied runic languages for a long time. Maybe longer than I should have." She blushed a little, embarrassed for some reason. But she happily pointed out the parallels between the runes she'd drawn and the ones on his hand, explaining in depth how her counter-enchantment would work. He didn't understand any of it. Many of the words she said were foreign to him, and the concepts were hard to grasp.

Eventually, she went silent, waiting for his reaction. He was at a loss for words.

It wasn't until that moment that he had understood how truly beyond him she was.

Perhaps mortals were right to think of demons as dumb beasts, because compared to her, he knew nothing of the workings of the universe. He had never studied anything the way she studied enchantments. Even if he'd wanted to, he could not read the texts she pored over. The symbols on the page held no more meaning to him than the runes on his palm. The idea that she could absorb meaning from the writing covering the page felt almost like magic in itself.

His own magic ability came from instinct, not from a true understanding of how the magic worked. It was like everything else he did—he was only good at fumbling his way through by brute force.

She was young for a mortal, but she had already learned so much and gained so much skill.

"You are very clever," he said softly. It was an entirely inadequate way to describe her.

"Oh. Thank you," she said, as if it was nothing.

"I thought you were a mere craftsman of enchantments, not an inventor of them. You have impressive skill."

"I don't know about that. But I'm glad I can be of assistance."

"You offer more than just assistance," he said quietly. "If

you were not with me, I would be trapped and without hope."

She looked surprised. After a moment, she reached down and put her hand on his. There was a feeling almost like sadness coming from her.

"I'm glad I can help," she said. "No one should be trapped or hopeless."

He curled his fingers around her hand, just holding it. Warmth enveloped him.

"What will you do after you're free?" she asked. "You said you will not return to the hells."

"No. I will remain here with you."

She blinked. "With me?"

There was surprise in her voice. Azreth went still. A cold feeling swept over him, extinguishing the warmth. He looked up at her, searching her face.

He had not thought about what would happen in the future, after she didn't need him anymore. Of course she would leave him eventually.

He pulled his hand away from hers. "Yes."

She looked at him closely. "What do you mean by that?"

It was like she was taunting him. She was challenging him to admit what he meant—that he'd thought they would stay together and help each other, and he hadn't thought about when that arrangement would end.

She must have thought he was a fool. And she was right. She must have been privately laughing at him for believing that she wanted his company or that she thought he was something more than a monster.

Suddenly he wanted to be cold to her. He wanted to make her feel what he felt. "You will stay by my side while I remain on your plane," he said. "That is all."

"That's all?"

"Yes."

She crossed her arms. "Perhaps you should ask me what I plan to do, instead of telling me."

"What do you plan to do?"

"I don't know. I hadn't decided yet, and I was considering my options."

If she left him, he would either have to force other mortals to feed him, offer himself to the disgusting cultists, or die.

She could take everything from him. Maybe it wasn't fair to her that he depended on her in order to live, but it wasn't fair to him, either. And besides that, the thought of her leaving him made that flame in his heart burn so hot that it became like a lump of iron in his chest.

Anger and fear made him increasingly stupid. Words spilled from his mouth before he could stop them. "You will remain with me, and I will feed from you."

She raised an eyebrow sharply. "Is that a command?"

"If it must be."

Anger billowed from her. It made him nauseous. "You can't do that. You can't tell me what to do. You're not my master."

"There is nothing you can do to stop me. You are weak."

Her jaw dropped. She slammed her book shut, and it seemed like she'd barely restrained herself from kicking it away before she stood up. "How dare you talk to me like this?"

He stood up too, so that he could look down on her. "You give me no choice," he said through his teeth, baring his fangs. "I must feed, or I will grow weak and die. There is no other option."

"Perhaps I would have continued to help you if you had just asked me. Did you think of that?"

"You said you were considering leaving me."

"So you've decided to force me to stay?"

"If you refuse, you will force my hand!"

"So if I tried to leave you, you would keep me against my

will? And how will you feed from me? Do you plan to hold me down and torture me?"

Was that what she thought of him?

Of course. Of course it was. Wasn't that exactly what he was threatening her with?

"I do not want to hurt you." Just the idea of it caused him a pain that was almost physical.

"Then what is your plan, exactly? How will you feed from me if I'm unwilling?"

He said nothing.

"I thought you—I thought we were getting along," she said. "You can't have it both ways. You can't have my trust and friendship while also holding me hostage."

"I apologize if I gave you the impression that you should trust me," he said. It wasn't what he'd wanted to say, but it was what came out, anyway.

"You're right. That was my mistake." The words struck him like a slap. She shouldered past him to move toward the hallway, and he grabbed her.

She looked back at him, apprehensive. Shame filled him, and he loosened his grip a little.

"Where are you going?" he asked.

"To my bed."

"It's only midday. You will not require rest for hours."

"And?" She gave him a challenging look.

"Aren't you going to try to undo my binding?"

"When I'm not feeling so exhausted, maybe." She glanced pointedly at his hand on her. "Release me." She looked like she wasn't sure he would.

He let go. He wanted her to understand, but didn't know how to explain himself. He wanted to throw himself at her feet and beg for her forgiveness. But he didn't. And she left.

SEVENTEEN

He found that the best place to avoid the cultists was the roof of the temple.

He spent the day watching the people on the streets below. They looked even smaller from so high up. The people of Ontag-ul never seemed to look skyward, which he guessed was because they didn't have airborne predators to look out for.

The sun beat down through the chilly air, warming the roof tiles, but the heat did little to improve his mood. The argument he'd had with Raiya replayed in his mind, even though he wanted to think of anything else.

He had never spent so much time thinking about another person. It was disturbing behavior, but he couldn't stop.

A shadow darkened the window behind him, and he was surprised to see Raiya there. Her expression dimmed when she looked at him.

"I'm ready to try a counter-enchantment," she said.

He raised his eyebrows—he hadn't thought she was still working on it. She'd been so angry. She still was.

She turned around and went back inside without waiting for an answer, and Azreth followed her.

She dropped her satchel on the floor in the center of the temple's stuffy attic, and a small cloud of dust floated into the cold sunbeam that cut through the window. "You'll have to provide magic for it," she said. "We should get that out of the way, first."

He felt both relief and disappointment at once. He'd been having a lot of strange emotions lately—feeling unhappy when he should have been glad, being relaxed when he should have been on edge, having strange combinations of feelings that should never have been combined.

"How shall I feed?" he asked.

She shrugged one shoulder, disinterested. "However you want to."

He wanted to feel a thrill at being told to do whatever he wished with her, but he felt only a vague unease. Kneeling in front of her, he looked up at her face, noting her serious expression. He wanted her forgiveness, but he didn't know how to get it. Perhaps now wasn't the time to ask. Or, perhaps he was just a coward.

Cautiously, he curled his hand around the back of her soft thigh. Her leg fit neatly in his hand, and when he squeezed, there was a pleasant give to it. He slid his fingers gently to her inner thigh, between her legs. To his relief, he felt a pulse of arousal from her. Maybe he could still make this enjoyable for her, even if she was angry at him.

But he still hadn't fed since they'd arrived at the temple, and he still didn't have the energy to cast spells. He only had one hand. "It is more difficult without magic," he admitted quietly. "Without my hands."

Her hard expression softened. "It's all right," she said quickly. "It won't be a problem. We've never had a problem before." She began to remove her trousers and underclothes.

His heart clenched painfully. Kindness came to her instinctively in the same way cruelty came to him, even after he'd hurt her.

He was determined to do this well, because at the moment, he couldn't seem to do anything else right.

"Will you help me?" he asked.

"Of course."

He took one of her hands and guided it between her legs. "Touch yourself."

She raised her eyebrows a little, and Azreth wondered if he'd committed yet another mortal faux pas. But then she did as he asked.

Her eyes remained locked with his as she pressed her fingers against herself. They bent and unbent slowly, summoning arousal like a mage gathering magic energy, and she waited until her desire had built to what seemed like an almost painful threshold before she slid them deeper, and then each stroke was drawing out small curls of pleasure. It was mesmerizing—beautiful.

"You are good at this," Azreth said. She didn't need him at all, really.

"At what?"

"Pleasuring yourself."

She stopped abruptly. "Are you making fun of me?"

"No."

"Isn't everyone good at pleasuring themselves? I mean, don't you ever...?"

"No."

"You don't? Or can't?"

"I don't like to."

She stared at him, frowning. Azreth averted his eyes. He gently took her wrist and pulled her hand back to her core, and after a moment, her fingers resumed their slow rhythm.

"Do you like it... with me?" she asked.

Reluctantly, he looked up at her and studied her face. She looked hopeful and worried.

"Yes," he said softly. "With you."

He ran his hand up the back of her leg, pulling her closer, and touched his lips to her inner thigh. There was a sharp spike of heat in the air. He parted his lips and tasted her skin and her slick.

He'd wanted to pleasure her with his tongue nearly from the day he'd met her, but he hadn't imagined it quite like this, with him on his knees before her, wanting her in ways he'd never wanted anyone.

The way she gasped when he drew his tongue over her sex, though—that was exactly as he'd imagined it. Startled, she bucked against him. He could still feel her stiff unease beneath her pleasure, but after a few more strokes, it was gone. Her hands, reaching blindly for him, landed on his horns.

Azreth jolted. Raiya curled her fingers tighter around his horns, holding him against her, unaware of the taboo nature of what she was doing. A shiver went through him. Being grabbed by the horns was cause for great offense in the hells, but this wasn't the hells, was it?

He grabbed her thigh and lifted it over his shoulder, then buried his tongue in her. She struggled to stifle a moan. Excitement and need burst from her, washing over him.

There was nothing uneasy about the way she grabbed him. She didn't ask permission or worry she would offend him— she simply moved him where she wanted him, demanding his service. And he was happy to give it. He was coming to the horrifying realization that for her, he would do almost anything.

THE COUNTER-ENCHANTMENT DID NOT WORK AS INTENDED.

Or did it?

For a moment, after Azreth charged the enchantment and was immediately racked with pain, he thought Raiya must have deceived him. Instead of ridding him of his binding, she'd branded him with an enchantment of eternal torture to punish him, and he couldn't even be angry at her for it. It was what he deserved. A part of him was pleased that she'd finally been wise enough to turn on him.

As he fell to the ground, writhing in agony, she climbed onto his chest. He thought of Nariel on top of him, strangling him, but then he saw her face. She was panicked, scrubbing at the runes she'd just painted on him.

Her counter-enchantment hadn't woven correctly, and as the spell tried to right itself, it was raking over his body and mind. His vision distorted as wild, uncontrolled magic sparked through him.

And then it stopped. He slumped on the floor, breathing hard. Black liquid that he at first mistook for blood drenched his chest. Raiya had dumped her entire bottle of ink over him to cover the runes on his skin, breaking the enchantment and stopping the pain.

Her eyes were wide with horror. "I'm so sorry. I didn't think it would be so bad if it went wrong. I've never tried enchanting a person before, and I didn't know…" She reached out to touch him, and when he pulled away, she looked hurt.

The flame in his heart snapped, like firewood releasing a flurry of sparks. He felt them rising into his throat, choking him. He couldn't take it.

He sat up and took her by the chin, turning her face up toward his. He stared at her eyes, looking for answers. There were none. He saw only deep, dark depths in their black centers.

All his emotion came out in a burst. "Why—Why are you this way?"

She looked startled. "What?"

"Why worry over me like a mother nyra?" he snapped. "Why cry when I am hurt? Why do you never use my weaknesses to your advantage? Do you not know what I am? Don't you know that I consume your kind for power? Don't you have any sense of self-preservation? Just yesterday, I angered you. I threatened you. But still, you worry for me. Still, you attempt to serve me. There is no logic here. I cannot understand it. You are the most baffling creature I've ever met."

"I didn't—I don't—"

"You should *let* me be bound. You should rejoice in my pain. It is a victory for you."

She frowned, affronted. "I've never wanted you to be in pain."

"But why?"

"There will never be a better explanation, no matter how many times you ask for it. This is just how mortals are."

"No. It is how *you* are. Only you."

He wanted to shake her, and hold her, and shout at her and cry in her arms, because he was doomed.

He was in love with her.

EIGHTEEN

It was rare for Azreth to spend time among other demons, but it did happen on occasion, for one reason or another. Sometimes, even for demons, there was safety in numbers.

He had passed through the vast desert on the east side of the forest of crooked trees only twice in his first seven years of life. He did it not because he particularly enjoyed having his skin abraded in sandstorms, enduring the ungodly heat, and running from massive tunneling beasts, but because he sometimes had no other choice. This time, it was because a group of older, more powerful demons had begun encroaching into what had been his territory, pushing him out.

As he was reaching the last of the trees at the edge of the forest, he saw two kin he'd never seen before. They stood at the top of the first dune beyond the forest, and they carried packs and belts laden with supplies for traveling, just like he did. They had already spotted him and were watching him, still as statues, their expressions hard.

He was surprised. Demons usually traveled either alone or

in larger groups, not in pairs. It was too easy for one to betray another in a pair. Many would not be able to resist the temptation.

They were outcasts, like himself—wanderers with no house affiliation. One of them was nearly as tall as Azreth, with large, curling horns, her skin and hair greenish in some places and deep amethyst in others, and she carried a deadly obsidian sword at her hip. The other one was very small for a demon, almost sickly. Her skin was deep, rich red, but her horns were tiny, protruding only a few inches from the crest of her forehead.

Both of them were smaller than Azreth. While he was confident he could best either of them in a solitary fight, the two of them together might be able to take him down. But he didn't think they would risk fighting him just for a chance to slake their bloodthirst.

It was an ideal situation for an alliance.

He straightened, making himself look as tall and powerful as he could, while not making any aggressive movements. He tried not to look like he was extremely hungry—which he was. If he looked too desperate, they wouldn't risk coming near him.

"I will accompany you across the desert," he said evenly. It was not quite a request, but not quite a command. Not too forceful, but not too soft. "We will be stronger as three."

The women exchanged a glance. One murmured something to the other. They spoke for longer than he expected.

The taller one turned to him. "Come, then. You will do as we command." She was testing him.

"I will not," he answered simply. He wouldn't fight them, but he wouldn't yield, either.

She looked annoyed, but not surprised. "Don't follow too closely. If danger comes, you will approach it first."

Azreth didn't reply. They had already started down the other side of the dune.

Their names were Basmeth and Atara, which he only learned when he overheard them addressing each other. They didn't ask his name.

Atara, the small one, always walked in front of Basmeth, putting the larger woman between herself and Azreth, who trailed some distance behind them both. Azreth meant her no harm, but he didn't take offense. Her caution was wise.

At first, based on their size disparity, he had assumed she was Basmeth's slave, but it soon became clear that wasn't the case.

Their behavior was strange. He did not often get to observe other kin, so he spent much of his time watching the two of them. They often spoke to each other quietly as they marched across the swollen dunes, arms held in front of their eyes to block the harsh wind and pelting sand. They walked close together, and they turned their backs to each other sometimes, unafraid of being struck from behind. Occasionally, one would touch the other's arm to get her attention, or to briefly lean on the other for balance, and it was clear they were comfortable with and accustomed to these small touches.

Once, Atara noticed him watching Basmeth, and she gave him a look of warning so fearsome that he averted his gaze without comment.

They did not invite him to join them when they fed from each other, but they allowed him to feed passively from nearby —which he preferred, anyway.

Basmeth liked to climb above Atara as a man might have, interlocking their hips while Atara lay on her back beneath her. She did not rush. Her movements were slow, hypnotic. Azreth could never see Basmeth's face during this, because she always turned away from him, but he could see Atara gazing up at Basmeth, looking her in the eyes. They traded soft, intentional touches, leaning in until their bodies were twined together. When they climaxed, there was an outpouring of passion and joy unlike anything he'd witnessed, but Basmeth was quick to get to her feet and turn away, leaving the smaller woman panting and alone on the ground.

Their relationship was almost embarrassing in its intensity and softness, and Azreth watched them with a morbid curiosity.

They were nearing the end of the desert when they encountered a flame geyser and stopped to take turns bathing in it. Azreth took his turn last, straddling the splintered rock from which the fire spouted in great bursts. As he stepped into the flame, the heat eased the aches of the days-long march.

He turned to where Basmeth and Atara sat nearby. He did not have to hide his gaze, because they were deep in whispered conversation, their faces somber. They sat so close together that their knees touched.

He went still when Atara abruptly wrapped her fingers around Basmeth's wrist—in his mind, a clear display of aggression. Basmeth just shook her head, as if it were not a threat at all, but their voices grew a little louder.

They were arguing. He hadn't seen them argue before. Fearing a fight would break out, he stepped out of the geyser. He had no interest in becoming involved in their quarrel.

But instead, Atara dropped to her knees, taking Basmeth's hand in both of hers in a supplicating gesture. With the flames behind him, he could make out her harsh whispers.

I need you.

I would do anything for you.

You know I feel...

He followed the movement of Atara's lips in disbelief, watching them shape damning words.

I love you.

Azreth stiffened. Basmeth recoiled in shock.

He had heard of enthrallment—the madness that mortals referred to as love—but he'd never witnessed it. Demons afflicted with it would find themselves lost in obsession and subservience to another for no logical reason. It was ultimate enslavement.

I love you.

The words filled him with disgust. Just looking at Atara, seeing her earnestness and willing vulnerability, made him angry. Why she had chosen to admit such a humiliating truth was beyond him. But if she was truly enthralled, then she was too far gone to think clearly, wasn't she? Maybe she couldn't help herself.

The lucky ones, the ones who had proven valuable to their eldresses, would be exorcised with a complex spell that would free them of emotion entirely. Even then, it had to be done by force, because the enthralled were so mad that they didn't *want* to be cured.

But the three of them were houseless. There would be no eldress magic for them, and there was no other way to cure it.

Azreth took a step back. Perhaps it was contagious.

Tears slid down Atara's cheeks. Suddenly noticing Azreth watching, her eyes narrowed a little. Basmeth followed her gaze.

For a moment—just a moment—he thought Basmeth might turn to Atara to proclaim her own enthrallment in return, because what else could have explained the way Basmeth shielded the smaller woman from danger, let alone all the gentle touches and long conversations?

Was it possible that their enthrallment was mutual? Was Basmeth equally sick?

But then her lips twisted into a scowl. Contempt emanated from her. She drew the sword at her hip. Without hesitating, she lifted it high and then drove it through Atara's chest.

Atara didn't even try to fight. She looked Basmeth in the eye, just like when they'd fed, and her arms stayed limp at her sides, and Azreth couldn't help but think she'd expected this outcome all along. She had been so lost to her obsession that she had submitted herself to Basmeth's judgment anyway, as if the consequences no longer mattered. She had lost all rationality and all sense of self-preservation.

Basmeth ripped the sword from her body, letting loose a gush of viscous blood, and Atara tipped over and collapsed in the sand.

Pain and misery suffused the air like the scent of a decaying corpse: rank, awful, addictive. Azreth knew when the life fully left Atara's body, because the scent of her emotions faded. And yet, the pain in the air remained. It changed, growing deeper, blacker. Azreth had thought the feelings were Atara's, but perhaps they were Basmeth's, too.

Basmeth spun to face Azreth, her face a mask of fury. "Is there something you wish to say?" she snarled, pointing the bloodied sword at him. She took a step toward him, but he spotted a slight tremor in her raised arm. "Do you think I will not do the same to you? To anyone? Do you doubt me?"

"No."

He looked at Atara's small, limp body behind Basmeth, and hatred filled him. He was disgusted by her smallness, weakness, and foolishness. It wasn't right for someone to be so pathetic. Everything about her was upsetting.

The grief in the air was turning sour on the back of his tongue. He felt sick. He was unwell. Their pain was rubbing off on him somehow.

A horrible thought came to him—the madness was catching after all. It was the only explanation for this disturbing, overwrought sensation, like a sudden knot of tension in his body.

He could not let himself become like Atara. That was the worst fate imaginable.

He backed away. Then he turned and ran.

Love was for mortals. Demons couldn't have these feelings.

NINETEEN

Azreth was enthralled.

He tried to put Raiya out of his mind, and that made it worse, because he found that it was impossible.

Wherever he was alone, he felt the lack of her. When he closed his eyes, he saw her in his mind. When it was quiet, he heard echoes of her voice, like an ocean in a shell. When the cultists approached him, he wished she were there to deftly disengage them. When he watched the city streets from the roof, he saw small, chirping birds, windows covered by lattice-work, and mothers carrying bundled babies; he could not observe anything in the mortal world without remembering the first time she'd helped him understand it.

Even his own misery was cause to miss her. He liked that whenever he was bothered, she would take his hand soothingly and tell him that all was well. He wanted that. It was pathetic.

As he wandered the halls that night, he imagined her in her bed in the sleeping quarters below. Was she thinking of him? If she was, she was probably thinking of how unkind and cold and dangerous he was. Why did it pain him to think about that?

It was all wrong. He shouldn't have been worrying about her abandoning him—it should have been the opposite. He needed to separate himself from her before it was too late. He had to stop this.

It was likely that he seemed a little desperate as he flung open the door to the living quarters, awakening everyone inside.

"Get out," he said to the cultists, who were groggily looking up from their beds.

"What?" one of them asked, rubbing his eyes.

"Get out," he growled. The cultists seemed to take note of his mood. They got up and quickly left.

He turned to Raiya. She was looking up at him confusedly, still covered by her blanket. Her hair was mussed and her eyes were heavy-lidded. She was beautiful.

He was going to tell her he was leaving, and that she would have to find someone else to protect her from Nirlan. He would go as far away as he could, to the other end of Heilune, so that he couldn't change his mind later and find his way back to her. He'd find some other mortal to feed from, and he'd find another way to cleanse his body of Nirlan's binding. Above all, he needed to be free.

He went to sit on the edge of her bed.

"Azreth?" she asked.

"I must speak to you."

"It's the middle of the night."

"I cannot wait."

Their past few interactions repeated in his mind over and over. The feel of her on his tongue, her hands on his horns, the heat of her and the sound of her soft gasps. Her knowing smile as she commiserated with him. The way she'd panicked when she'd thought she'd hurt him. The threats he'd made, the way she'd started when he snapped at her, and the hurt on her face when he'd treated her like an inferior.

He paused, gathering his strength. He opened his mouth, and somehow, what came out was, "How do your people show remorse?"

Raiya raised her eyebrows. It wasn't what either of them had expected. Azreth clenched his hands in his lap.

All this time, he'd been worrying about Raiya betraying him, but he'd betrayed himself in the end. She'd trapped him with kindness instead of cruelty.

Why could he not will himself out of it? Why could he not even make himself try?

"What are you remorseful for?" Raiya asked.

"Injuring you when Nirlan fed you to me. Taking you from the castle by force. Frightening you. Threatening you. Forcing you to serve me." The list was long. He could have gone on.

She frowned a little. "You didn't force me. This was a mutually beneficial arrangement from the beginning."

"I knew you had no other choice."

She said nothing. Maybe she sensed the truth in his words.

"I would never have hurt you," he said. "When I said I would, I was lying. I would not keep you against your will."

A silence dragged.

Then Raiya leaned closer to him. "You're nothing like what they say, are you?" she said softly. "Demons are just like anyone else. You think and feel just like we do. You're just trying to live. You're not monsters. You're not evil."

It was the last thing he'd expected her to say—but maybe he should have known better. This was just the way she was.

"Are we not?" he asked. "What is a monster? What makes something evil?"

"Hurting people. That's evil."

"I hurt people. I hurt you."

"Do you think you're evil?"

"I wouldn't know."

"How do *your* people show remorse?" she asked.

"In the hells, penance is paid through submission and servitude. If I wished to align myself with someone I had previously offended, I would put down my weapons and prostrate myself before them so that they could punish me or feed from me. I would offer myself to them to use however they wished." If she asked that of him, would he do it? He probably would.

"Have you done that?"

"Not willingly."

She frowned. "I see."

"My people express regret when they want something from someone. Apologies are made for diplomatic reasons. But that's not what I want. I feel regret because... I'm afraid I have been cruel."

There was another silence. Raiya was studying him, measuring him.

"I don't think you're cruel," she said, more gently than he deserved. He glanced over at her skeptically.

"Tell me what service you require in order to forgive me," he said.

"An apology is enough on its own, as long as it's heartfelt."

That did not seem like enough. But he supposed he could keep trying to make it up to her. He would never be as kind as she was, but he would keep trying for as long as she would let him. "Then... I apologize."

"I accept your apology."

It was that simple. She had removed all his anguish over their argument with a single sentence. Such was the enormous power she held over him. It was terrifying.

"Do you really think demons can feel all the things that mortals can?" he asked.

"Why shouldn't they?"

"We are made different. Look at you. Look at me." He took her small hand, looking down at her earthen skin. Vibrant red blood pulsed through her veins. She was nothing like him. Mortals and demons were not meant to coexist. They were naturally opposed. One must always conquer the other.

But she looked down at his hand calmly, as if she didn't notice how grotesquely large it was compared to hers, or how damaged by battle and defeat it was, or how the thick muscles and tendons implied the potential for violence. She turned his hand over and ran her fingers lightly over his palm. Pinpricks ran up his spine.

"There are more similarities between us than differences," she said.

He brought his hands to her face, cupping her cheeks. She went still, surprised.

He realized he'd come to her because he was afraid. But how could he seek comfort from her when she was also the reason for his fear?

He dragged his hands away from her. "I'm sorry for disturbing your rest," he said, and he left.

"LAST NIGHT," Priestess Gereg announced, "I had a vision. In it, I saw the demon before us. He spoke with the dark goddess's voice and proclaimed that he had come to fulfill Moratha's plans for Heilune. He is to be a reaper, come to bring her wrath upon our plane. He is her instrument of death, a weapon of unknowable destruction. It begins tonight. There will be a massacre of epic proportions, starting right here in Ontag-ul. All will die. Humans and elves, children and animals alike. Death will rule the land, blood will flow like water, and Moratha will be pleased. So, demon: thus begins the goddess's reign. You are commanded to kill indiscriminately, whenever and wherever you desire, so long as it is often. You will rend flesh with your monstrous hands, tear bloody gashes with your terrible teeth, crush bones beneath your giant's feet. Go now and destroy. Spare none. We will follow in your footsteps with our blades high!"

Then the priestess had the audacity to bow to him, pretending respect.

Azreth had guessed it would come to this, but he had hoped they would find a solution to his binding, first. They'd run out of time.

From where they stood by the altar at the front of the main hall, they'd have to push through a wall of cultists in the pews in order to reach the exit.

Raiya seemed not to know what to do. Azreth sensed that she wouldn't be able to smooth talk them out of harm's way this time. He moved closer to her, ready to put himself between her and the others, because he guessed they wouldn't be happy with his response to all this. Her hand was already on the handle of her baton, but that wouldn't protect her thin skin from a stray blade or spell.

"No," he said simply. He almost enjoyed the look of faint surprise on the priestess's face. He could tell that people didn't often say no to her.

"You are refusing her call?" she asked, her tone warning. He didn't care.

"I am."

She gave him a haughty look. "You were designed by the dark goddess to serve her will. You will obey her. It is your purpose."

"What do you know of my purpose?"

"You are a tool to be used as she decrees for the spreading

of darkness and despair. You are death. This is your purpose, just as a stock animal's purpose is to feed, as a mother's purpose is to nurture, as a wheel's purpose is to roll. It is not a decision to make. It is already done."

He had thought he was above emotional outbursts, but the priestess's words sparked something in him. He surprised himself and everyone else when he raised a fist and slammed it down into the altar, smashing it into several large pieces. Beside him, Raiya jumped, and he felt a pang of regret. She was the only person in the world who believed he wasn't a monster. She was wrong, but he still cherished her faith in him.

"What do you know of my purpose?" he snarled at the priestess.

She just blinked, unfazed. "Do you deny your goddess?"

"I care nothing for your goddess."

The cultists gasped. Finally, the priestess looked angry. This would be the final straw. Raiya sensed it, too. She grabbed his arm and began to pull him down the aisle toward the doorway.

"You *will* serve her," Gereg called after them. "If you will not do it willingly, then we will break you. You will obey." A commotion broke out among the cultists. Gereg was shouting something. People blocked his way.

Azreth took Raiya's hand, pulling her against and behind him. "Get out of the way, or I will send you to your goddess," he snapped at the cultists.

There was a swell of magic energy in the air. A powerful spell was being cast.

By the time he sensed it, it was already too late. A wave of energy passed over him, and then a magical barrier encircled him. It cut Raiya off from him, separating their hands. The sounds in the room grew muffled.

Azreth raised a hand to the barrier. The wall was transparent, but completely solid to his touch, just like the cage Eunaios had placed him in.

Dread filled him. He pounded on the barrier. Nothing happened.

Raiya was looking down at the floor beneath him. She kicked aside the long rug that ran down the aisle, and carved into the floor was a circle of runes from which the barrier had sprouted. A trap. He'd walked into a trap. Again.

He had underestimated the cultists. He'd grown too comfortable around mortals, and he'd become complacent.

Outside the barrier, the cultists surrounded Raiya. He watched them put their hands on her, pulling her away from him.

"Stop!" he shouted, pointlessly. No one heard him, or no one listened. Raiya elbowed the cultists away with surprising strength and then pointed her baton at Azreth, at the barrier. He flinched as magic exploded against it—but it remained unmarred.

"Destroy the runes!" he shouted, pointing to the floor. Raiya's wide eyes followed his gaze. She aimed the baton, but before she could shoot again, one of the cultists grabbed her. Spells and blades flashed as Raiya twisted away from them. Azreth pounded against the barrier uselessly, furiously.

Through the jumble of bodies, he spotted the baton again, raised high in Raiya's hand. It glowed bright, then shot a blast at the ceiling.

There was a shower of dust, then rubble. People scattered, covering their heads. A corner of the room collapsed with a crash, and the room was entirely obscured by a cloud of dust.

When the dust cleared, Raiya was gone.

Azreth's heart pounded, silence echoing in his ears. The walls of the barrier seemed to close in, though they did not move. He watched the exit at the end of the hall, where Raiya must have run.

She was gone.

The sense of loss that filled him was a physical hollowing, like something had been torn out of his body and left along with her.

"Go after her!" Gereg said sharply, her voice muffled by the barrier. Several people were already out the door, but he didn't think they'd catch her. Somehow, he sensed she would be all right. An empty, cold calm came over him.

Priestess Gereg's hood had fallen down during the fight, and her hair and makeup were mussed. Another cultist dutifully began rebraiding her long hair for her. Gereg still looked furious, which pleased him.

She turned to leer up at him, her eyes roving over his body in a way that made him feel disgusting. She was admiring him —thinking of what she would use him for.

"You'll do as your goddess commands you," she said to him.

"I have no goddess."

"Do not insult the dark lady in her own temple!" she hissed.

He enjoyed making her angry. It was all he had now. "Your goddess is nothing."

Everyone gasped.

"Don't say another word," Gereg said, her voice low and dangerous. The edges of her face, the parts where the paint had worn away, were turning pink.

Azreth had never really tried to insult someone before. He wasn't sure how to do it, so he simply said the worst things he could think of.

"Your goddess is weak and ineffectual," he sneered. "I would spit on her."

The cultists gasped again. Some of them shouted arguments back at him.

"I do not find her beautiful or strong or good," he went

on. "I do not respect her. I look down on her as I would an insect."

Someone threw something at him—a bit of rubble. Several more followed suit. He ignored them.

"A so-called goddess who wants only death?" he shouted at them. "She creates nothing, builds nothing? Does she see nothing, too? Hear and feel nothing?"

A mage tried to levitate a set of manacles through the barrier. Azreth grabbed them out of the air and hurled them back into the mage's face. The man fell to the floor and didn't move as other concerned cultists crowded around him. He might have been dead—it was difficult to tell.

Iron, the crowd inevitably began to murmur.

"Your gods have given you everything," Azreth said to them. "You are born healthy and safe and free, to caring families in thriving cities. You could make art, or learn crafts, or read every book in Ontag-ul. You could travel everywhere and learn every language. You could create life, raise children or animals, or just dance and make love all day. You are not demons—you are free of this bloodthirst, this need to *feed*. You have the freedom to make anything of your lives, and instead, you crave *unmaking*? You crave a *lack*? Where is the beauty and cleverness in undoing things?"

Now the cultists looked more confused than angry.

He turned to Priestess Gereg. "You are spoiled, small children, and your god is a god of nothing." He did spit in disgust, then, which he'd never done before, but he'd seen a mortal do it once, and it had looked like it would feel gratifying. Spittle hit the barrier and stuck there. Gereg gave it a look of distaste.

When the first iron chain came levitating through the barrier, he grabbed it, ignoring the raging burn of it against his skin, and whipped it back at the cultists. They ducked this time. One of them caught the chain in another levitating spell. Several of them worked together to push the chain back toward him. Petulantly, he threw it away again and again, until the iron had burned so much that he could no longer feel his fingers. There was no point in fighting. He wouldn't escape them. He just wanted to hurt them.

Eventually, they maneuvered chains around him, and he was encased in agony. The iron sapped his strength, turning his limbs to liquid, and his legs went out from beneath him.

By the time they lowered the barrier, he could hardly see straight. The intense wrongness of the iron was almost as bad as the pain itself. It was an ugly, wretched thing, like an itch he couldn't shake off, a horrible bitter gag stuck in his throat, insects crawling under his skin. It was overwhelming, blocking out his surroundings, so he was only vaguely conscious of being pushed and pulled through the hall.

He saw a dark staircase before him, very much like stairs into a dungeon beneath a castle, and it was as if he'd never escaped Nirlan at all.

TWENTY

It was odd how cruel mortals could be, wasn't it?

They had no need for it the way demons did. They simply enjoyed causing pain. Azreth had always thought that kin were uniquely perverted in their desire to cause pain and misery, but demons and mortals were more similar in that respect than he'd ever imagined.

He was kneeling on the floor, unable to stand. Candles flickered around him, barely illuminating the small crowd in the temple's cellar. The iron on his skin burned, and burned, and burned. He wondered whether it would kill him before the cultists did. Could a person die from pain alone?

Perhaps he should have thanked them for saving him from the enthrallment, at least, since he hadn't had the strength to save himself.

"I thought a demon would be more difficult to subdue."

"It looks like a stray dog, shivering like that."

"Should we kill him? Would the dark goddess be pleased?"

"Of course she would. She can't love a creature this weak."

He recognized the Priestess's voice when it cut through

the murmurs. "You cannot be a true demon," she decided. "You lack the heart for it."

Azreth struggled to raise his head. His vision was blurred. For a moment, he saw the eldress in front of him. Then he blinked, and she was gone.

"AZRETH?"

A familiar voice cut through the pain, distant and very close at the same time. He shifted slightly, but his body felt impossibly heavy. The iron seared him when he moved.

"Azreth?"

And then her face appeared in front of him. It must have been a dream, but it was a painfully realistic one.

"Raiya?" he heard himself say, the word a hollow breath.

"It's okay. I'm here. You're safe." Her voice was soft, but her eyes were furious, powerful. Her cool hands were on his cheeks, holding him, and he wanted to sink into the illusion.

Raiya's face disappeared, and then magic swirled around him. The world tilted, and then he felt cold.

A weight began to lift off him. Slowly, the vise grip of the chains released, unraveling link by link.

Was he dead? Maybe this was the afterlife. In that case, there must have been a kind goddess watching over him.

The temple was gone. He was lying on his back on the ground. Above him was the vast expanse of the black mortal sky dotted with stars, and Raiya's pale, lovely face.

He reached for her, wrapping his arm around her to pull her against his body. He breathed deeply, inhaling the warmth and mortalness of her. The scent roused something from the depths of his soul—something that was starving.

Energy and life pounded through him, ravenous. All of it came at once—the need to feed, the relief at seeing his mortal, and the desire to hold and taste her. He burned from the iron, but something burned inside him, too, scorching him from the inside out.

Flesh called out to him. Blood begged to be spilled. Wounds wanted to be opened.

Regaining strength, he rolled over and pinned the mortal to the ground by the throat. He pressed his mouth to her shoulder, and he savored the explosion of fear and pain as he sank his teeth in.

She screamed. The sound was a knife cutting through his mind, and he froze.

He held her there like the predator he was, trapping her with his teeth. She had gone still. Somewhere in the back of his mind, he realized he should have released her, but that thought was quickly lost in a spiral of hunger, and he lapped the blood from her skin.

Stars burst across his tongue. She tasted like fire, like bliss. He sucked at the wound, needing more of her. Her blood was sweet and ripe, her skin smooth and soft against his tongue, and he realized he had never truly eaten before now. The most meticulously cultivated fruit in the world would not compare to this.

He imagined he was licking between her legs. In his mind's eye, he saw her moaning in pleasure, her body wrapped around his as he drank from her.

And then he realized that he wasn't entirely imagining things. Her body was still strained against him, but now she was pulling him closer instead of pushing him away.

"Azreth, say something," she begged.

For a second, he wondered who Azreth was. The world came into slightly sharper focus.

He dragged himself away from her throat to look down at her, and his blood pounded through his veins so hard that his vision shook. Raiya was looking up at him with wide, shimmering eyes. She arched against him, her hands balling into fists where he'd pinned them to the ground. He realized that he'd summoned a dozen hands to hold and touch her, without even meaning to. Through the hands, he could feel all of her at once—her soft hips, her gently angled jaw, her lightly muscled thighs and fine-boned wrists—and it was both too much and not nearly enough.

"I want you," he said breathlessly, but those three small words could never convey the longing and desperation he felt in that moment.

He felt her desire intensify. An invisible thread seemed to form between them, and it pulled him, drawing him to her. She nodded urgently.

His need for her built into an overwhelming force, clouding his mind, and his body moved almost without thought. His summoned hands flipped her over, pulling her against him. He found the small, tight warmth between her legs, and suddenly there was nothing more important in the entire universe than being inside that warmth. Lust had never been in his nature, but now he ached with it.

Closing his eyes, he sank into her. Her body stretched to take him, but he heard her make a pained sound. He snapped to attention again, looking down at her. She was wincing with the effort of accommodating him.

He bent over her, hugging her to him as he covered her sex with his hand and spelled her, opening her body. She sighed with relief, sagging into his hands.

"*Gods,*" she murmured. "Gods, *please.*"

He pushed deeper into her, and she moaned in pleasure, a sound that might have been the most lovely thing he'd ever heard in his life. He felt the pressure of release building in her body as his hips rolled against hers in a mesmerizing beat. His hands closed around her thighs, pulling her against him until there were no gaps between them. When she cried out again, her climax soaked into him, thick and sweet. It drove him over the edge. Light exploded behind his eyes, blinding euphoria.

He hadn't known it could be like this. He'd never known it was possible to feel this kind of joy. Was this what sex felt like for mortals? Was this what making love felt like?

The sounds of her rapture echoed through his mind. He was bewitched by those sounds, and he felt a strange sense of pride over being the one to cause them. He loved giving joy, he realized. He loved pushing her to the limits of pleasure and then pushing even further.

He could have lay beside her and inside of her for ages. He wanted that. He wanted this to be forever.

He dropped his face against the side of her neck, feeling her pulse beneath his lips. "You came back for me," he said, disbelieving.

"Of course I did," Raiya said simply, as if there had been no other possibility.

And then he smelled the fresh blood from where he'd bitten her. A chill went through him.

It was like a bucket of icy water thrown over him, sobering him instantly. Disgust sank through him, settling into the pit of his stomach.

He turned Raiya onto her back, setting her down in the grass. She looked up at him guardedly, her eyelids heavy. The bite beside her throat was shallow, but not shallow enough. It had not been deep enough to put her life in danger, but it would probably leave a scar. The thought made him ill.

He wove a spell over it, and it sealed over with new pink-brown skin. Only time would tell how much the marks would fade.

He knelt on the ground, pressing his forehead against the grass. "I lost myself. I did not mean to hurt you. I beg your forgiveness."

"Forgiveness?" she asked, as if she didn't know what he meant.

If someone had done to him what he'd just done to her, he would have tried to destroy them. But she accepted it as if she thought she deserved it.

Because she's used to it, said a voice in the back of his mind. Nirlan was her mate, and he hurt her. She was accustomed to being dragged into bed and hurt. It was the one thing she'd asked him not to do. *I don't want to be bruised or bloodied.*

He hated that he'd done this. He hated that this was what he was. He wished she had sharp teeth to bite him back. He wanted to be hurt.

"I have broken the terms of our agreement," he said. "Strike me, and I will lie still while you pay the hurt back."

She just scoffed. "I don't want to hurt you. I will never hurt you."

"I cannot say the same."

"I don't believe you." She put her hands around his face and drew him up, then pressed her mouth against his. Azreth tensed, anticipating a bite.

But he never felt her teeth. Just her breath mixing with his. She was soft and warm and gentle, her lips lax but full enough to give a slight pressure. She stayed there for a long moment, and he remained perfectly still, his heart in his throat. It would be so easy for one of them to inch forward and ravage the other with teeth.

It was intoxicatingly intimate. He had a strange urge to open his mouth and taste her, but he didn't move. He'd done enough to frighten her already.

Finally, she broke away, still holding his face. The look she gave him was one of utmost trust and affection, and he nearly broke.

Mortals and demons should not be together. Raiya deserved better than Azreth and his violent urges. But he couldn't bring himself to leave. With every day that passed, he was further gone than before. Before he'd met Raiya, he would never have allowed anyone to touch him this way. He would certainly never have enjoyed it.

His enthrallment pressed him to throw himself at her feet again. *Let me serve you forever*, he wanted to say. *I am yours.* It took all of his willpower to stay silent, but he knew he couldn't last much longer. He was a slave to the enthrallment. To her.

He wove another healing spell, lowering his hand toward her thighs. "Are you hurt here?"

"I'm fine, Azreth."

He hesitated, his spell pulsing slightly on his fingertips as it waited to be applied. "I know you are strong," he said slowly, not wanting to offend her. "I do not offer this because I think you are weak. I offer it humbly, as a service to you. Please accept—as long as it doesn't displease you to have me touch you."

She looked bemused. But after a moment, she nodded. "If you wish."

She held still as his hand moved between her legs—almost, but not quite, touching her. He hovered there, using the spell to sense the damage, then pushed the magic past her skin. Her inner thighs were hot and slick when his fingers brushed against them.

Raiya swallowed audibly. When he glanced up to meet her eyes, she looked down. "It... feels better," she said, nodding.

With her encouragement, he gently flattened his palm upward, cupping her body to pour the spell into her. He heard her inhale softly in surprise. Soothing magic sank into her.

For the first time, he glanced up to try to work out where they were. They were in a dark field he didn't recognize, outside of Ontag-ul. He had no idea how they'd gotten here.

"How… did you do this?"

"A teleportation enchantment. A shortcut through the aether to move from one place to another." Exhaling softly, she lifted her arms around his neck, leaning against his chest. "I was afraid I wouldn't get you back," she said, very quietly.

His heart burned.

"Inside," she whispered. "Please."

He slid a finger just past her entrance, stroking her softly but making no effort to urge her toward climax again. He was no longer sure whether he was healing her or pleasuring her, but it didn't seem to matter. Her arms tightened around him, and she rocked slowly against his palm as she embraced him.

TWENTY-ONE

Raiya was incredible.

Azreth was astounded by the teleportation enchantment she'd made, even though she called it sloppy work. Perhaps other kin knew of this magic, but he'd never seen its like. On top of that, she had fought her way into the temple and through the cultists to get to him. She'd even convinced several other mortals to help her rescue him—her night elf Roamer friends, Jai and Madira, and (to his mingled confusion and annoyance) Adamus, the Paladin they'd set free on the road, whom she'd run into again in the city.

When she'd left Azreth in the temple after the cultists trapped him, she hadn't run to save herself. She'd immediately gone back to the Roamers, demanded assistance on his behalf, planned a rescue, recruited help, and produced a powerful enchantment to shift him out, all in a matter of hours.

Azreth imagined it over and over, thinking of how angry and determined she must have been to have done all that for him. He pictured her storming into the camp and shouting orders, mercilessly blasting through cultists with her baton, thinking of him all the while.

Something shifted between them after that night.

The change was mostly in him, if he thought about it. Raiya had always been kind to him, always smiling at him, always offering him her hand. He was the one who had maintained the barrier between them.

When she asked him to return with her to the Roamer camp just outside of Ontag-ul to visit Jai and Madira, he agreed easily, despite his mixed feelings about the place. He followed wherever she guided him, not just because he had nowhere else to go, but because he trusted her wisdom and because he wanted to see her smile when he said yes. He was an obedient pet, a vigilant bodyguard, and her shadow. He would go anywhere with her, do anything she asked.

Succumbing to the enthrallment was terrifyingly easy. He slipped beneath the waves of desire and trust, drowning himself. He was fully broken, and the longer it went on, the less he cared.

If he'd been enthralled by another demon, he would have been doomed—thrown on his back and ruthlessly used, or exorcised, or simply executed in disgust, like Atara. But with Raiya... perhaps he would live through this.

The Roamers welcomed them into their midst again. Jai and Madira offered them a bedroll, even after it became clear that they realized what he was.

He knelt beside Raiya as she tucked herself into her bed. Rain pattered against the walls of the tent. Outside, there was a burst of laughter from a group of Roamers who were still awake. Azreth pictured them smiling and laughing, enjoying each other's company.

He had hated them before. Their joy had made him furious. Now, he thought nothing of it. He was not even annoyed by the noise. He was embarrassed by how he'd reacted to them before.

Raiya's hair was freshly washed and damp, shining in the

lantern light, and the skin bared by the collar of her undershirt was clean and smooth. Through the thin, white cloth of her underclothes, he could make out the faint shape of her body, all supple and slim and curved. When he looked at her, he had an urge to touch her that was completely different from anything he'd felt with another person before. It was nothing like the dull, obligatory attraction he'd felt toward Nariel, and he didn't know why.

"It's been a while since you slept," she said. "You must need rest."

"Not here."

She smiled gently. "No one will hurt you here. And I'll be with you."

A dull pain cut through his chest—the enthrallment. Before now, he hadn't known that enthrallment presented not only as an ailment of a mind, but as a physical sickness as well. His chest ached constantly. When she was sweet to him, it got worse. He had never loved pain so much.

"I can't." It wasn't that he didn't trust her—only his own fear held him back. He would never be able to sleep while he could still hear dozens of people in other tents nearby.

"Then will you just hold me while I sleep?" she asked.

"Are you cold?"

"No."

He looked at her for a long moment, glancing toward and then away from the healing bite mark on her shoulder. "Does it not frighten you to have my arms around you? Does it not make you feel... trapped? In danger?"

She smirked, amused. "I like having your arms around me."

There was a painful twist in his heart again. He slid closer to her, looming over her, but instead of shying away, her eyes went soft and sweet.

"Do you know that you're beautiful?" she said.

She must have meant to say something else. No one had ever used the word *beautiful* in relation to scarred, disfigured Azreth. But she slid her hand over his arm, savoring the feel of his skin as if it were luxurious fabric.

"I suppose you must know that you're impressive," she said. "And I suppose demons are designed to seduce mortals, so maybe it goes without saying. But you're beautiful. I'd bet that you're uncommonly beautiful even among other demons."

The pain in his chest throbbed, so intense he thought he might die. He took her hand, and then he was leaning down, putting his face close to hers. He paused with his mouth an inch away from hers, almost thinking better of it, because maybe she'd misspoken or maybe he would frighten her or maybe he wasn't doing this right.

But then he leaned in and carefully touched his lips to hers, the way she'd done to him before. A thrill went through him, from his head to his toes. It was reckless, transgressive, deviant. It was a spectacular display of trust to invite someone's mouth and teeth so close.

When he finally broke away, he did so reluctantly. "I am happy to do as you ask," he murmured.

She seemed slightly breathless. "Happy?"

"Yes."

Since she'd removed her outer clothing before bed, he did too, and then he slid into bed behind her. The space was so small that he was forced to press against her, bending his body around hers. She balled herself up against him, pulling his arm over her waist as if she saw it as a source of comfort rather than a weapon.

As he was about to enter their tent the next evening, he overheard his own name. He stopped just outside the door flap, listening. Raiya was speaking to someone inside.

"Don't ever let a suspiciously handsome, rich man court you, Jai. It's not worth it."

"What about a suspiciously handsome, rich lady?" It was Raiya's young elf friend. Azreth could hear the cheeky grin in her voice.

Raiya paused. "Fair enough. If you can find a nice elf girl, I'm sure you'll be better off. But don't let anyone bully you into falling in love with them, either way. And if someone hurts you when they're angry, don't believe them when they say they'll never do it again."

For once, Jai didn't fill the heavy silence.

"It doesn't seem so bad at first, when you're still blinded by love and you still believe it was a one-off event. But it's never just a one-off. Once he realizes he can take his anger out on you, he'll do it every time. You'll start to worry about any little thing that might upset him, and... It's not love after that. You'll feel like a hostage."

Azreth heard something shifting, perhaps one of them moving to touch the other.

"Just be careful," Raiya finished quietly.

"Raiya..." Jai said hesitantly. "Don't you ever..."

"What?"

"I mean, he's a *demon*," Jai whispered.

Azreth closed his eyes, almost a flinch.

"Didn't he keep you hostage?" Jai asked. "Hasn't he hurt you, too? Isn't he dangerous? How can you be sure it's not the same as it was with your husband?"

Raiya sounded darkly amused. "He's certainly more bloodthirsty than Nirlan ever was."

"That's exactly what I mean. I almost thought you hadn't noticed."

"Oh, I've noticed."

"Then what's the difference between him and Nirlan?" Jai asked.

Raiya was quiet for a long time. Azreth was on pins and needles, his heart heavy. He almost turned around and walked away, but he couldn't bring himself to move. He knew Raiya would try to defend him, even though Jai was right, and that pained him. He imagined her weakly protesting that he wasn't that bad, that he had only hurt her a little, as if that made it all right.

In the end, she said something he hadn't expected.

"Azreth believes mortals are different from demons," Raiya said finally. "They're not, but that's what he believes. He thinks mortals think and feel more deeply than he does. I think he thinks about that a lot. He wants to understand us—to understand me. He wants to know what I'm thinking and feeling, and why."

"Oh," Jai said, but it sounded like the younger girl was having trouble following. Azreth was, too.

"Nirlan never thought about my thoughts and feelings," Raiya said. "I don't know if it occurred to him that I had any."

"Oh."

"The real difference is... I chose this. And I'm happy. My life is not spinning out of control anymore. I'm choosing where I want to be, what I want to do, and who I want to do it with. I'm not the same person I was when I was rotting in that castle."

"That wasn't long ago. How much could you have changed already?"

"I don't know how to explain it. It's like something snapped. I don't know who that person was, but it's not me. Not anymore."

"That's good. I think?"

Raiya laughed a little. "It's very good."

Azreth relaxed a fraction. He pushed aside the tent flap and stepped inside. Jai and Raiya were lounging on the floor of the tent.

Jai jumped. "Oh, hello, Azreth!" she said brightly.

He looked down at her. To his amusement, she just smiled at him, as if she had no misgivings about him at all.

He couldn't dislike someone who worried over Raiya as much as he did.

ON THEIR THIRD night with the Roamers, Raiya persuaded him to sit with her and the others around their bonfire while she ate dinner.

Jai had been persuaded by the group to sing while musicians played their twanging stringed instruments. She'd been sipping sweet cider all evening, and her face was glowing blue-black in the firelight.

When the song ended, she laughed and quickly sat down. She covered her face as the group applauded, but she was still smiling. He could feel her mingled pride and embarrassment from where he sat.

Azreth had never been young, exactly, but he had spent his first year of life in constant fear and confusion. There had been no joy. Not like this. He envied her.

But he knew now that it wasn't as simple as that. Young mortals were carefree and happy, but also sensitive and contemplative. Their emotions were intense. Jai was usually smiling and laughing when she was among others, but more than once, he'd seen her sitting alone with tears welling in her eyes. The first time he'd seen her that way, he had watched her for a few minutes, then approached her.

"What happened?" he asked.

She looked up at him, startled, and a tear dripped down her cheek. She quickly wiped it away. "Nothing."

He moved closer to examine her. "Are you hurt?"

"No." She sniffed and smiled a little. "Are you worried about me?"

He had never felt a protective urge toward anyone but Raiya, but he found himself wanting to help Jai. He didn't like seeing her upset and alone. "If someone hurt you, I will make sure they don't do it again."

"No one hurt me." She shook her head. "You wouldn't understand. Did Raiya tell you to come over here?"

"No. She is with the shepherds."

Jai sniffed, crossing her arms. "Ironic that the only one here who cares about me is the demon."

He frowned, perplexed. "But everyone here loves you."

"No they don't."

For a moment, he wondered if he had greatly misunderstood the other Roamers' behavior toward Jai. But then he realized that she was the one who was mistaken. Perhaps she even knew it, deep down.

He knelt beside her. "You must keep moving," he said. "You must not give in to despair. A mortal life is too short." She gave him a narrowed glance, and he sensed her flare of irritation, but he went on anyway, raising his eyes to the hills behind them. "I was asked to fetch water. Can you show me the way to the river bank?"

"It's right over there. It's not hard to find."

"Please show me."

She reluctantly got to her feet and stalked in the direction of the river.

Gradually, her bad mood faded, and soon she was smiling and chattering as they walked, even though Azreth could still sense a sadness hidden in her. A lot of mortals had that sadness buried deep within them.

WHILE RAIYA USED her research from the temple's library to work on developing another counter-enchantment for his binding, Azreth had free time, which was something of a novelty. He spent much of that time watching the other people in the camp. At first, he'd watched out of wariness, but after he grew more comfortable among the Roamers, it became something he did merely out of curiosity.

He realized he could tell which people were mated by watching whether they went into the same tent at the end of the day. He watched those ones particularly closely. The happiest ones seemed to spend a great deal of time together and touched each other often.

He couldn't help but notice that he and Raiya did both of those things, too.

The pair he was most curious about consisted of a young, pale human boy and a dark-skinned girl who spent much time together but still seemed shy around each other.

From what Raiya told him, the two were in the midst of some kind of courting ritual. They both wanted to be together, but they could not tell each other that they both wanted to be together, even though they both knew that they both knew they both wanted to be together... Or perhaps Azreth hadn't understood it correctly, because that seemed too convoluted to be feasible.

He watched the two of them sit together by the bonfire one evening. They talked for a while, and then the girl pulled a paper package from her pocket and presented it to the boy. The boy looked surprised, but pleased. He opened the package to reveal a strip of something small and colorful.

There was a burst of delight so powerful that it made Azreth squint. The boy stared at the object, practically glowing with happiness.

"I made it for you," the girl said. She sounded almost apologetic, but Azreth sensed her pride. She took the strip—a dozen different colors of thread woven into an intricate pattern—and tied it around the boy's wrist. It was only a bracelet, but they were both trying and failing to suppress grins.

When they left the bonfire circle later that evening, they walked away hand in hand.

Azreth glanced down at the bracelet on his own wrist.

THE NEXT MORNING, he looked around the camp until he found a set of woodworking tools to borrow, then took them to a wooded space away from the tents to begin working. He searched the woods until he found a suitable branch, then propped it against a stone as he shaved bits of it away.

He successfully hid the project from the rest of the camp until it was almost complete.

"What's that?" asked someone behind him.

Azreth stiffened in surprise, but he recognized the voice. Jai's brother, Madira, had managed to sneak up on him. According to Raiya, this was something night elves had a talent for, so he tried not to take it personally.

"It will be a bow," Azreth said.

The night elf came around to his front, stepping into the dappled sunlight beneath the trees. He crossed his arms as he watched Azreth work. His green eyes were as bright as a demon's. Raiya had told Azreth that some mortal scholars believed elves and demons had been made by the same gods, from the same mold. Azreth found the idea ridiculous.

"That's way too small for you," Madira scoffed.

Azreth didn't reply.

"It's for Raiya, isn't it?"

He sighed a little. Mortals were too good at guessing things he didn't want them to know. "Don't tell her."

"It's a surprise?"

The word had negative connotations. It made it sound like something alarming and dangerous. But technically, it was true. He didn't like to lie to her, even by omission, but he wanted to see the look on her face when he presented it to her. He hoped she would be pleased.

"How romantic," Madira said dryly.

"Is it?" Azreth said without looking up.

"No. You're just trying to make her like you." When Azreth didn't reply, he needled, "Do you think she'll bed you if you give her this?"

Azreth was surprised that he hadn't realized she was already bedding him. The question amused him. Madira amused him, generally. The boy pantomimed aggression all the time, but there was no real aggression in him.

"You should speak more," Madira said.

"Why is that?"

"Because it's strange when someone speaks to you and you don't say anything back. If you really want to pass as a mortal, you should act like one."

"Perhaps there is nothing important to say, or perhaps your question does not merit a response. Perhaps more mortals should be like me. Some of them talk a lot."

Madira shot him a glare. He came closer, eyeing the decorative designs Azreth was carving into the bow's limbs. "Why is everything so square? You should carve some flowers on it. Ardanian women like flowers."

"Raiya is not Ardanian."

"You know what I meant. Human women."

Finally, Azreth paused. He wondered if the designs were ugly.

He liked the geometric shapes because he'd never seen

them in nature. The straight lines and symmetrical angles could only be made by the hand of a living being, and he found that beautiful. But what did he know about art or beauty, really? Maybe she wouldn't like it.

"Why are you doing this?" Madira asked, his eyes narrowed. "Are the two of you...?"

Azreth didn't know exactly what he and Raiya were, but he knew that they weren't a real couple like the ones he'd watched around camp. A mortal could not marry a demon. She would never call him her husband.

But he wanted her to look upon him fondly. He wanted to be the cause of her happiness.

He put himself at Madira's mercy, because he had no other mortals to ask. He obviously couldn't ask Raiya, and something told him that Jai would have a difficult time keeping a secret from her. "Would it be... wrong, for me to give her this?" Azreth asked. "Would she take offense?"

The elf gave him a long look. Then he rolled his eyes. "I suppose it doesn't look that bad. And she will probably enjoy it either way. She acts as though everything you touch is gold."

"She does?"

Madira just rolled his eyes again.

Something moved above them, and Azreth looked up. A large, black bird, larger than any other avian creature he'd yet seen in the mortal plane, flew silently above the trees. He tried to follow its path through the sky, but the branches obscured his view and he lost track of it.

He realized that the forest had grown quiet. There was no birdsong. Hairs rose on the back of his neck.

"What is it?" Madira asked.

Azreth waited another moment, listening, then shook his head. "Nothing."

TWENTY-TWO

The peace could not last forever. It should not have surprised Azreth when the hells came back to haunt him, but it did. He was by the woods with Raiya, watching her practice with the bow he'd given her, when it happened.

The sound of the vythian was instantly recognizable. At first, he thought he must have misidentified it. Vythians were creatures of the hells, and there was no way one could have found its way to the mortal realm.

But then he saw it, and there was no mistaking it: a massive, black-scaled, flying beast with teeth like daggers and fire shooting from its maw.

He had only seen a vythian twice before, and both times, he'd managed to lie low and avoid their notice. This one was rapidly moving closer, toward the camp, toward the peaceful behelgi herd, and toward Raiya.

A group of kin might have been able to take down a vythian—but just him alone? It was impossible.

As the Roamers began to scream and run for their lives, he took Raiya's hand and ran alongside them. They detoured to find Jai and Madira, and then the four of them rushed out of the camp. When the vythian torched a line of tents beside them, Raiya jolted, leaning into him. They kept running.

"We must get to the city and behind something solid," he said to her, raising his voice to be heard over the screams and roars.

"And when it sets fire to the town?" she asked.

He didn't have an answer.

They were only halfway to the city wall when he heard the vythian diving close behind them. It gave a screech so loud that it vibrated his insides against his bones. Raiya covered her ears as its massive shadow fell over them. Fire was like iron to mortals. If the flames even came close to her, she'd be hurt.

He jerked her against him, bending close to shield her. The vythian swooped over them without touching them, but the gust generated by its wings was strong enough to make him stumble. The creature circled away, but it would be back.

He pulled her behind a building just outside the town gates. They panted there for a moment, and no one spoke, not even the elf siblings who always seemed to have something to say.

He leaned around the corner of the building to watch the nightmarish scene unfolding. Tents on the far side of the camp were ablaze and fire was creeping through the grass, already spreading. The behelgi herd split up as the animals ran for safety. People were fleeing in disorganized panic, some of them in states of undress, many dragging children or elderly behind them or carrying handfuls of valuable possessions. Only a few had picked up swords, but he couldn't fault the others—there was no point in trying to fight.

He looked back at Ontag-ul's walls, his heart sinking into his stomach. The wooden city would burn like dry brush, just like the camp, if the vythian's fire got to it. People and animals would die by the dozens. There was no place to hide.

He looked down at Raiya. Her eyes were bright with anger, her cheeks ruddy. She looked up at him hopefully, and he realized it was the same way he often looked at her. It was a request for guidance.

The look startled him. He was not used to leading.

The vythian was a foreign danger to them—one they were not equipped to face. Azreth was not equipped for it either, but there was no one else who could fight it.

It would have to be him, or no one.

Channeling magic, he summoned his wings. He felt them sprout from his back, felt the magic filling them out, and then felt the air beneath them as they became solid. He flapped them once, testing them as he stepped out from behind the building.

"Where are you going?" Raiya asked, her tone rising with worry.

Perhaps he should have confessed his love to her then, before it was too late, but he didn't. Going quickly felt easier than lingering and saying goodbye.

Without looking back, he sprang into the sky and flew toward the vythian. The sounds of the panicked crowd and the crackling flames faded beneath him as he took to the air.

It took him a while to cross the space to the vythian, and for a long few moments, he was flying alone in the quiet. It gave him time to think about how very foolish this was. But he already knew he wouldn't change his mind.

He didn't think he could win this fight, but maybe he could at least trouble the vythian enough that it would reconsider its choice of prey, or weaken it enough that the mortals could finish it off.

The vythian was turned away from him, facing the scattered behelgi herd. As it reared back its head for a blast of fire, Azreth folded his wings and dove, accelerating rapidly.

He crashed into the vythian's neck, knocking both of

them sideways. He clung onto it as it flailed, then bit into its neck. The hard scales scraped his teeth like steel on stone, but he crunched through them and reached flesh just before the vythian managed to throw him off.

The vythian's blood coated his mouth, tasting like acid and rusted metal. He spit out a mouthful, but the acrid taste remained.

He rushed toward the vythian again, this time aiming for the membrane of its wing. The creature roared as he cut through the delicate flesh, but before he could dive at it again, its massive tail whipped toward him and hit him like a rock wall.

He did not remember falling, but suddenly he was on the ground, his entire body ached, and it hurt to breathe—a rib injury, he guessed.

The ground shook in a quick rhythm. Enormous footsteps.

Azreth shoved himself to his feet. Dragging its torn wing, the vythian was galloping toward him, jaws agape, getting far too close too quickly, and suddenly all he could see was a mouth full of teeth as long as his forearm—

A burst of magic like a bolt of lightning struck the vythian, making it stumble. Azreth stared at it in confusion, then looked toward the city gates. Raiya was standing with her baton beside the building where he'd left her, drawing attention to herself instead of taking cover. He glared at her in warning, and she shot him a glare right back, but to his relief, she hurried back behind the building.

Vythians must have been stubborn creatures, because this one seemed to have no interest in retreating, despite its wounds, and only seemed to have gotten angrier.

At least it was grounded, now. As it turned its attention to Azreth again, he wove another spell.

This time, instead of wings, he made a sword. It was bigger

than any weapon he'd ever summoned, longer than he was tall, which felt appropriate for what might be his last battle. It floated above him, and when he moved his hands, the sword moved with him, like an extension of his body.

He backed away as he struck with the sword, swinging and stabbing as he would in a duel. The vythian growled in annoyance as it snapped at the sword with its teeth, all while continuing to slither toward him. The sword barely slowed it down. The magenta blade scraped and clanged against its tough scales, rarely finding a spot weak enough to penetrate, and though Azreth was keeping out of reach of the vythian's teeth, he was still on the defense, and the spellcasting was quickly draining him.

He was so preoccupied with his swordsmanship that he didn't spot the telltale glow in the vythian's mouth until the fire was coming at him. He didn't have time to do more than flinch, covering his face with his arm, before it engulfed him.

A vortex of unimaginable heat whirled around him, deafening. When he inhaled, fire burned down his throat and into his lungs. He stumbled, pushed back by the force of the flames, and he felt the mortal-made fabric around his shoulders shrivel into ash.

He wondered, for the first time in his life, if there could be a fire so voracious that even a demon would burn.

Eventually the fire slowed, then stopped. The vythian had run out of breath.

Azreth slowly lowered his arm away from his face, trembling. Letting the glamour fade, he looked down at himself. His skin smoked. The enchanted bracelet on his wrist glowed bright red. His boots and sarong were scorched black, but intact. He stood alone in a streak of charred dirt, all the grass and plants around him gone.

As he looked up at the vythian, he allowed himself a

moment of foolish pride. He was losing this fight, but he was not finished quite yet.

The vythian lunged. Azreth dove sideways as he brought the sword down, barely evading the vythian's charge. His body had grown heavy, and the threads of magic that maintained the summoned sword were fraying. As he struck at the vythian again, he stole a glance in the direction of the behelgi herd behind the camp. They were gone, hopefully somewhere safe. The camp was empty. Everyone had evacuated. Hopefully he'd bought the warriors and mages in Ontag-ul enough time to gather weapons and plan some kind of defense. And hopefully Raiya was hidden deep in some cellar, far out of reach of the vythian.

Abruptly, his strength failed. He lost his grip on the spell, and his sword disappeared, leaving him open to attack.

The vythian didn't hesitate. It darted forward, its long neck stretching as it opened its mouth wide. Azreth ducked, but too slowly.

Jaws closed over him. Teeth sank through his skin, like half a dozen swords at once. He did not even have the strength to gasp or cry out. The teeth sank deeper.

He was going to be cut in half. What a messy way to die.

The shock ebbed, and for a moment, feeling returned to his limbs. He jabbed a hand toward the vythian's head. Raking his fingers across its face, he hit upon something soft that tore in his grasp. With a shriek, the vythian released him and backed away, swinging its head in distress. One of its eyes was gone.

Azreth dropped to his knees. Blood gushed from a row of tears along his torso.

"Hey!" someone shouted.

Azreth looked up. So did the vythian. They both turned toward the voice, toward the slight figure that was approaching from the city.

It was Raiya. She was running straight toward the vythian. Azreth's heart nearly stopped. He paused to wonder whether he was hallucinating, because it looked like she was brandishing a long stick with a jangling sack tied to the end of it.

"That's right," she shouted, waving the sack in the air like a war banner. "Leave him alone!"

To Azreth's horror, it did as she asked. It ran toward her, and—and she ran to meet it. She had gone mad. The vythian raised its head above her. It opened its mouth, ready to strike.

And then, like some kind of avenging eldress warrior queen, Raiya hefted the stick high and thrust it deep into the vythian's mouth, where it stuck.

The vythian stopped, its neck convulsing. It shook its head, trying to dislodge the stick caught in its throat as Raiya backed away.

Azreth didn't fully realize what she'd done until the vythian began to retch. Thick, greenish steam poured from its mouth, and its screeches became strange, heavy gurgling sounds, like its insides were melting.

It was iron. She'd force-fed it a sack full of iron.

He'd thought being bitten in half would be a bad way to die, but this was worse. Much worse.

It was mercifully quick. The vythian fell to the ground with an earth-shaking crash, then went still.

Stunned, he looked at Raiya. She looked back.

She had killed a vythian.

She'd remembered its weakness and had used her mortal nature to her advantage. Azreth couldn't have made an iron weapon to kill it, but she could. Even with all the strength and magic at his disposal, she had still outfought him.

She was incredible. And right now, she was rushing to meet him, tears in her eyes, like he was the most important person in the world.

"Azreth! That was foolish of you to fight that thing alone. Damn you, that was foolish."

"Are you hurt?" he wheezed.

"No!" she snapped, as if she disapproved of him asking. She fawned over him, nervously hovering her hands here and there as she surveyed his wounds. "You saved everyone. The whole camp. The whole town."

"The behelgi?"

She made a choked sound. Her emotions were vast and heavy. He couldn't quite tell if she was laughing or crying. She looked over her shoulder to check the herd. "They're fine. They're all fine."

By the city, there was a crowd watching. Hundreds of mortals were gathered near the gates, staring at him. At a dying demon. A few pointed at him, lifting weapons.

He had been willing to die fighting the vythian, but he did not want to fight the mortals he had begun to feel close to in these past weeks, and he did not want to look into their hateful eyes as he died, now that they'd discovered what he was. He didn't want to be hated.

He looked at Raiya, suddenly less resigned to death. He didn't want it this way, not here, not by the hands of the people he'd only wanted to help.

"Help me," he asked Raiya. He realized it was something he'd never asked anyone before.

A stray tear spilled onto her cheek. She nodded quickly, helping him up.

She helped him run as far as he could—which, it turned out, was only a few dozen strides before he collapsed in the grass again. He was bleeding heavily, and he was dizzy and lightheaded from the loss of blood. Raiya knelt over him and compressed the worst of the wounds with both hands. He winced as pain pounded through him.

"Do you trust me?" she asked.

"Yes." Of course he did. Nearly since the beginning, he had, even if he hadn't wanted to.

"I'm not going to let any of them harm you. I will die before I let that happen. So worry about keeping still and conserving your strength, not about them." She looked him in the eyes, her gaze fierce, and she was beautiful. She was a vythian killer—she feared no mortal.

When the first mortals caught up to them, Azreth tensed, but they did not attack. It was a group of Roamers, and they approached warily, and then they healed him.

He looked up at Raiya for reassurance as a Roamer woman wove magic into his injuries. There was an uncomfortable silence as the woman worked and other Roamers stared at him openly—with curiosity, not hatred.

Strangely, that pleasant pain in his heart flared. He had thought Raiya was the only one who could trigger that feeling.

When the vythian had come, he could have picked up Raiya and fled, leaving the others to their fates. He was glad he hadn't. These people were worth defending. This place, the mortal plane, needed to be protected.

And right now, it needed to be protected from whoever had brought the vythian here from the hells.

Nirlan had summoned Azreth from the hells, so it stood to reason that he could bring other things here, too. Was he vindictive enough to call something as destructive as a vythian to his own homeland?

What would he bring next, if no one stopped him?

TWENTY-THREE

Azreth and Raiya left Ontag-ul with the Roamer caravan, eager to put the cultists and the dead vythian behind them.

The Roamers celebrated every night, drinking and playing games and laughing late into the evening. Raiya, wearing a cheeky smile, had given Azreth a cup of bitter liquor to drink, and then another, and then another. No matter how much he drank, he did not feel the same dizzy pleasure from it that Raiya and the others did.

There was nothing to celebrate that night, or any other night—it was just what the Roamers did. Raiya told him this was normal for humans.

"Why not?" she said with a shrug. "We're mortal. Every day might be our last. I think we should make the most of it."

He puzzled at that. Demons lived every day like it might be their last, too, but in a different way. "Does that frighten you?" he asked.

She thought for a long moment, then looked up at him. "Everyone fears death. You do, too, don't you?"

"Yes. But my death is... not so inevitable." Demons had

such fraught lives that they rarely survived long. But under the right circumstances, Azreth could have lived for eternity. Raiya would never have that option, even if she were cautious. Thinking about it made him hurt.

"Believe me, we are very aware of the inevitability of our deaths," Raiya said with dark amusement. "Especially humans. We're the shortest-lived race in Heilune, and everyone else makes certain we don't forget it."

"I'm sorry." He didn't know what else to say. It was the one thing he couldn't protect her from.

"I didn't mean you should be sorry. Everything ends eventually. But just because it ends doesn't mean it never happened. Dying doesn't mean that we didn't live. It can't take away our memory, or the marks we've left on the world."

She'd put into words what he'd already begun to understand about mortals: their mortality was why they spent years raising children, spent decades perfecting their crafts, and spent generations building great cities. Demons lived merely to live, but mortals lived to leave their mark before their end.

LATER THAT NIGHT, in their tent, he lay beneath her on his back—a submissive, vulnerable position that somehow didn't feel submissive at all with her. She was checking his bandages. The wounds he'd sustained from his battle with the vythian had mostly healed already, but she touched him with utmost care anyway, as if afraid of hurting him. He could have told her that he was fine and she needn't have worried, but he didn't.

She peeled back the bandage over his shoulder, where the worst injury was, and she winced as if the wound were her own. Azreth liked watching her as her hands explored him. His heart, in a permanent state of tension these days, clenched as she dipped her fingers in a salve and smoothed it over his skin.

After the vythian attack, he thought about Raiya's mortality more and more often. When she had charged toward the beast with only a broken broom handle in her hands, he'd been certain she was about to die.

She was young by mortal standards. She had plenty of time left. But he found it difficult not to think about it.

"How do you want to die?" he asked.

She raised her eyebrows, bemused. "Are you plotting something I should know about, Azreth?"

"No." He reached out to touch her face, holding her gaze on him. "You must have thought about it before."

She pulled out of his grip and focused on his shoulder, her expression solemn. She was afraid after all, then. She disliked thinking about it as much as he did. He took comfort from that, because it meant she realized the gravity of her situation. A part of him had wondered if mortals simply lived in denial to preserve their sanity.

"What about you?" she asked. "Have you thought about how you'll die?"

"I always thought I would die fighting another of my kind sooner or later. It's how most of us die. But now I'm not sure. Maybe a Paladin will kill me, instead."

"Or maybe no one will."

"I would want to do it myself, if I were mortal."

She squinted at him. "Do you mean... you would want to kill yourself? You'd want to die by suicide?"

"Yes."

She shook her head, grimacing. "You are so strange."

He didn't understand what was strange about it. "I would not want to be surprised by it, if I had the choice. I would not want it to be out of my control."

She pushed the lid back onto the jar of salve and began

wrapping new bandages around him. "Most mortals don't want to end their own lives," she said. "Most of us hope to die naturally when we're very old, surrounded by people we love."

"Surrounded? Why?"

"So we don't have to be alone when we go. Dying is not an easy thing. It would be scary and sad to do it alone."

He waited for her to finish wrapping the bandage. She tucked the edge of it into itself to secure it. Azreth sat up.

"I want to be with you when you die," he said.

She didn't speak for a long moment, and Azreth wondered if it had been an inappropriate thing to say.

"It's not easy to watch someone die, you know," she said.

"I'm not a fool, Raiya. I know."

"Sorry. I know you're not."

He reached out to take her hand. "If you let me, I will help you. I want to be one of the people surrounding you." He wanted to hold on to every last moment with her. But would that be enough for her? Could a demon offer the comfort a mortal needed to die peacefully?

"Do you think you'll still be here by then?" she asked. "Won't you have grown tired of me?"

He didn't know quite how to address such a silly question, so he just said, "No."

A warm, sweet-smelling emotion emanated from Raiya. She interlaced her fingers with his and squeezed his hand.

———

THE VYTHIAN WAS NOT the last creature from the hells they saw. They heard rumors of more in other parts of Uulantaava, too. As they traveled north with the caravan, they saw it for themselves. People fleeing Frosthaven told them that the creatures were coming from the lord's castle—from Nirlan.

The more Azreth thought about him, the more disgusted he became.

There were other people who had made him suffer more than Nirlan had, but no one else had been as pointlessly cruel. He could not understand what would embitter a mortal man so much that he would reach into the hells to bring violence to this peaceful place. People like Lord Han-gal and Priestess Gereg had no need for more power, but they were greedy for it anyway.

With Nirlan's creatures already attacking, they did not have the time to fix Azreth's botched binding first.

He and Raiya were in agreement that her ex-husband had to be dealt with now, but the binding wouldn't let Azreth kill him. Raiya would have to do it. He wasn't certain she was ready for it.

A permanent line had appeared between her eyebrows since the vythian attack. The scents of anger and worry came off her like steam. When she thought about Nirlan—which was often, now, he sensed—she became withdrawn.

She was so similar and yet so different from the woman he'd first met in Nirlan's castle. She had been just as brave and defiant when she'd first freed him, but she hadn't had the self-assurance she had now. She had her enchanted baton at her hip—a weapon she'd made for herself, which gave her the power to choose the course of her life instead of having it chosen for her. But each time she used it, he saw a conflicted look in her eyes, because she was still gentle at heart.

"You've changed, too, you know," Raiya told him.

"How so?"

"You're not always on edge, the way you were when we first left the castle. You were so angry and afraid. You're more at peace now."

Azreth thought back. Had he been on edge? Afraid?

Yes, he supposed he had. The fact that Raiya seemed to

know more about his emotions that he did was as humbling as ever, but it didn't surprise him anymore.

The mortal plane was no longer a strange and terrifying place to him. When he was with Raiya, it felt almost like a home—a home he wanted to defend.

"We're both stronger than we were," she said. "We're stronger together. I'm glad you're here, Azreth. Some things are easier when you're not alone."

He had realized that, too.

With each hour that passed, the desire to confess his enthrallment to her grew more difficult to resist. He wanted to submit to her fully. He wanted to be hers. It was grotesque. This was truly madness.

He thought of Basmeth and Atara often, lately. Back then, he hadn't understood why Atara would put herself in that position. The intensity of her feelings had frightened him.

He wondered how often Basmeth regretted what she'd done. Knowing what he knew now, he suspected that she thought of it every day.

He understood Atara, now. He needed Raiya to know how much he cared for her, even if she disapproved.

One night, Raiya laid him down beneath her in their tent, gently took him in hand, and coaxed him to completion, simply because she wanted to give him joy. There was no pain or regret in his mind as she touched him. He felt no humiliation, no weakness. He only felt love for her. That was when he decided he couldn't hold this secret any longer.

"There is something I must confess," he whispered as she ran her hand through his hair.

"What's that?"

He forced himself to look her in the eye. "In the hells, there is an illness of the mind—a rare and deadly kind of madness that befalls some of us. I have felt the change coming over me for some time. I am not myself. I can no longer think properly. I can no longer reason. I care only for one thing. It occupies my mind every waking second. I have tried, and I cannot escape it. The obsession consumes me."

Raiya was watching him closely, perfectly still. "What are you talking about?" she asked, but she knew.

"I have let myself become addicted to you," he said, watching her eyes sharpen. "I think of you always. I crave the feel of your skin and the sound of your voice constantly. Every moment I am away from you feels empty. Where I once would have cared only for myself, I now care for you. It's torture, and bliss. In the hells, the people who fall victim to this curse are called enthralled. Once the madness takes hold, it rarely lets go."

It was disturbingly easy to tell her everything. He often found himself unsure of what to say, but not now. The words came naturally. They were words he'd said in his mind many times already.

"Are you describing love, Azreth?"

He nodded slowly. "Yes. This is what mortals call it."

She looked at him for a long moment, her emotions a confused jumble. She looked wary. Worried. He didn't want that.

He reached for her, taking her arms. He was almost afraid she would run now that he'd confessed this sin, and he couldn't stand to think of her leaving him.

"Don't be afraid," he said. "This means I'm yours. Your servant. Your slave. Be anything but afraid."

She took his face in her hands, pulling him closer. "There is a difference between the devotion of love and the devotion of a servant, Azreth. Love isn't about power and submission and fear. When you're with someone who loves you back, like I do—" A swell of emotion interrupted her for a moment. She swallowed hard. "When you're with someone who loves you back, it's about mutual affection and trust and selflessness. It's the greatest thing in the world. People live for that kind of love. People kill and die for it."

"It scares me."

She slid her hands around the back of his head and put her lips close to his. "If you are mine, then I'm yours, too."

Azreth felt faint. Raiya's mouth touched his.

I'm yours, too.

His arms encircled her. He was a whirl of feeling as they fell to the floor and removed clothing. He had no coherent thought except for wanting to be closer to her, to be one with her.

Pure need flowed from her as she wrapped her legs around him. Soon she was trembling, her hips lifting and her core flexing as she took him inside her over and over. That line between her eyebrows was more prominent than ever as her face tensed with concentration. He watched her press her lip between her teeth and then release it.

"Bite me," she said.

The world seemed to shake. He pulled back a fraction. "What?"

"I know who you are," she said breathlessly. "What you are. I want all of you. The sweet parts, and the vicious ones."

For a moment, he was ashamed. She thought he was vicious.

But she was right. He was vicious. And she accepted him that way. She *wanted* him that way.

He wanted to be as gentle as she was, but he also wanted to taste her blood. There was a part of him that always craved violence; the thought of it made his blood run hotter. Violence was power and control and excitement. But *inviting* violence was a show of trust, and that thrilled him.

He bent closer to her, breathing in her warm, human scent. "I would never hurt you."

"I know," she replied, her eyes heavy-lidded with lust.

"I am yours."

"I know."

Cradling her, he tipped her head back to bare her neck. He had never thought that a bite could feel like an act of worship, but as he sank his teeth into her, that was what it felt like. Like he was praying at her altar.

Her body jolted. Her climax came like a crashing wave. Her fingers clenched on him and her body writhed. A rush of delicious, heady passion washed over him, mixing with the metallic taste of her blood. He pressed inside her and held her hips flush with his, so deep that they were like one body undulating in unison.

Maybe enthrallment wasn't madness, after all. Maybe it was the rest of demonkind who were mad.

He would be her willing slave—but he didn't need to be. They would belong to each other. Equals.

As Raiya slept in his arms that night, he looked down at his marked palm, watching the way the runes shimmered persistently in the light. It was the only part of him that still needed fixing.

IT BEGAN to snow as they reached Frosthaven, which seemed appropriate given the town's name.

Azreth was surprised to discover that snow was not merely frozen raindrops. They were not hard and painful, but light and fluffy, like little feathers. They floated on the breeze and gathered on roofs and in doorways like sand. It was soft and beautiful, like so many other parts of the mortal world.

Raiya ignored it except to pull her hood over her head. Her thoughts were elsewhere.

The four of them—himself, Raiya, Jai, and Madira—were alone on the town streets. Azreth began to think the entire place had been abandoned until he spotted a few sets of eyes peering out from behind curtains in dark windows. Even through the walls of the houses, Azreth could occasionally feel a beat of fear from within. The townspeople had all retreated behind closed doors—not that it would do them any good if more monsters came.

Jai was gazing around the empty, snowy streets. "This is your home?" she asked Raiya.

"It was."

"Not anymore?"

Raiya took a moment to think about it. Her eyes had a dull, regretful look. "I'm not sure."

"Home is where your friends are," Jai said. "A real home is wherever you choose to make it."

"That's not true," Madira said. "Kuda Varai will always be our home, no matter how long we spend away from it."

"Well, maybe Raiya doesn't want this to be her home anymore," Jai pointed out. "The place where you were born isn't always the place that feels like home. Especially not when you're no longer safe or welcome there."

Azreth watched Raiya, following the exchange carefully. She looked up at him as she answered them. "You're both right," she said, giving him a look that he couldn't quite interpret.

The signs of the demonic presence in the town grew more obvious as they went. Raiya led them up the streets past groups of velravens and the occasional mortal corpse. Azreth stiffened when a familiar scent hit his nose. It was hot and herbal, like dust and old magic and death.

It smelled like home. The fourth hell.

He looked up toward the source of the scent. On a hill just outside of town was the castle. It was different now. Even from this distance, he could sense the hell's mark on the place. It teemed with magic, and with that familiar dry scrubland scent. It was the last place a mortal should have dared approach.

"What do you want to bet that's where they're coming from?" Raiya said dryly, leading them toward it.

There were no other mortals until they came upon a group of Paladins who had come to fight the beasts from the hells. Azreth was somehow not surprised to see that Paladin Adamus was among them, because Adamus seemed to have a knack for ending up wherever they were. Nor was he particularly surprised when Raiya accepted his offer to accompany them to the castle, because she was far more trusting than she had any right to be.

That was all right, though. He trusted her, even if he didn't trust Adamus.

As they passed the castle's outer wall, he took Raiya's hand. It was something he never would have done when he was in the hells. The open display of affection would signal a weak point to anyone who saw. But it was worth it for the little burst of warmth and sweetness he caught in her scent when he touched her.

"Are you afraid?" he asked her.

"Of course," she said, giving him a rueful smile. "Are you?"

He thought about it, and he was surprised to realize that he no longer felt a sense of growing panic when he looked at the castle.

Enthrallment was supposed to be a disease of emotions, wasn't it? So why did his emotions feel more in balance now than they had during all his time in the hells?

"No," he replied finally.

"I wouldn't judge you if you were."

"I know."

She smiled up at him, but the expression didn't quite reach her eyes.

"We will succeed," he said. "Don't worry."

"Are you so certain?"

"I am certain that I will do whatever it takes to keep you from harm."

She squeezed his hand, her small fingers lacing through his. "I'll do the same for you."

They stopped in front of the castle's front doors. They were shut tight, a circle of glowing runes emblazoned on the dark wood. Adamus and the elves tried the doors and found them locked. Fortunately, Azreth had prior experience dealing with locked doors.

Without further ado, he kicked the doors down.

TWENTY-FOUR

The castle was quiet.

The others seemed surprised by the silence as they crept into the entry hall, but Azreth wasn't. Many creatures of the hells would lie silently in wait before striking. If he were one of Nirlan's minions, he would wait in the shadows until his target turned their back to him.

On the floor in the center of the entry hall, they found a human corpse. As Azreth summoned a sphere of mage light to illuminate the room, Raiya approached the body, leaning in to examine it without getting too close.

"It's Priestess Gereg," she said.

Azreth raised an eyebrow. "She's dead?"

"Quite dead." Raiya's mouth stiffened into a line. Blood was smeared all around the body. It was still fresh, not yet dry. The scent of it made Azreth salivate.

He was pleased. "Well. She's with her goddess now."

Raiya looked up at him, smirking. "Was that a joke, Azreth?"

"Maybe."

Madira poked at the body with his sword, turning it to

view the large gashes in its stomach. His nose wrinkled. "Do you think a sword did that, or another demon?"

"I cannot say," Azreth said. "We should find the lord and ask him."

Paladin Adamus kept his distance from the body, as if it were contaminated by some contagious evil. "A summoning gone wrong? It's hardly rare for a demon to kill its own summoner." He glanced up at Azreth. "No offense."

"The truth does not offend me," Azreth replied. Raiya gave Azreth a reproachful glance, as if she resented the implication that he might betray them. She trusted him so deeply that merely acknowledging this truth—that all demons were dangerous—offended her.

"The summoning circle the last cultist made was in the tunnels below the castle," Raiya said. "We should start there." She stepped around the dead priestess, and he followed close behind her.

The scent of decay tainted the air. They passed twisted, dead forms of more velravens and a thresher—more inhabitants of the hells brought here by Gereg and Nirlan. The bodies bore the same strange gouges they'd seen on Gereg.

Azreth made a mental list of things that could cause this much carnage but were also small enough to fit through the castle's halls. The list was not very long. His fingers fiddled with threads of magic at his side as he peered into every shadowy corner they passed.

The only thing he wanted to face less than a vythian was another demon. The vythian had been bad, but at least it wasn't intelligent.

The corridor opened into the massive room at the center of the castle. Azreth recognized it. The last time he'd passed through, he'd left it strewn with the bodies of mortals who'd tried to stop him from leaving. The bodies were gone now, but the room was not much cleaner for it. None of the lamps were lit, and the fireplace was dark. Cold air blew through broken windows while moonlight glinted on their broken glass.

There was rustling from above them, and Raiya came to a quick stop. Azreth put a hand on her shoulder as he raised his sphere of mage light higher. It floated to the ceiling, casting light on dozens of dark shapes in the rafters. More velravens. They seemed to be sleeping.

"Just birds," he murmured to her. "They're small."

"They're quite large by our plane's standards."

"But not bigger than I am."

Just as he spoke, the creatures moved. They awoke in unison, and there was a great fluttering of dozens of wings as they took off. Raiya ducked. Azreth raised a hand to summon a sword, then he realized the birds weren't attacking them. They flew in all directions, out windows and down hallways. They were fleeing.

Hairs on the back of his neck stood on end. "Something frightened them," he said. Raiya glanced up at him, shifting nervously.

Suddenly, it was deathly quiet. Even the wind seemed to have stopped, as if nature itself feared whatever was coming. Azreth listened to the silence, staring deep into the shadows around them.

Behind him, something moved.

He spun, putting himself in front of Raiya. Waving a hand, he summoned a magical shield. No sooner had it appeared than a beam of magic impacted the shield, blowing it to pieces. Azreth stumbled back, but another attack was already coming. He raised the shield again just in time for a second blast to hit it. He forced more magic into the shield, and this time, it didn't break.

He looked beyond his shield long enough to see a demon approaching them—long enough to feel a pang of dread as he realized that the other demon was much larger than himself.

As the demon launched another knifelike shard of crackling magic at him, Azreth rushed forward, shifting to one side to deflect the shard with his shield. He caught a glimpse of the demon's expression—faint surprise—just before Azreth slammed into his knees. His weight knocked the demon off his feet, and they both went tumbling across the floor.

Azreth wouldn't last long if they took to wrestling on the ground. He tried to roll to his feet, but a clawed hand swiped at him. As he grabbed the other demon's wrist and leaned back to avoid his claws, the demon arched over him, trying to pin him. Azreth jabbed a fist into his chin, knocking him off balance long enough to flip him with a twist of his thighs. With the demon under him, he swung an arm to gather magic into the shape of a blade, and in the same motion, he drove it toward the demon's throat.

The other demon was fast—much too fast. Before the blade could make contact, something flashed through the air and hit the side of Azreth's head, knocking him to the floor.

He rolled to his feet, bracing for another attack. The other demon was already standing, watching Azreth impassively, his posture relaxed. He had *allowed* Azreth to get up. Otherwise, he would have been dead already.

All of it had happened in a matter of seconds, but his heart was already racing and his muscles were burning from exertion. The mortal plane had spoiled him. He'd almost forgotten what a fair fight felt like.

Panting to catch his breath, Azreth studied the demon. He was taller than Azreth by at least a head, and his fingers were tipped with long, tapered claws. He was probably older than Azreth, but his crimson skin bore few scars, as if he'd not lost many fights. It went without saying that he wasn't missing any limbs.

When he looked closely, Azreth saw runes glowing very

faintly all over his body, catching the light whenever he moved. Nirlan had succeeded in binding him.

Azreth guessed the demon would have happily killed them even without Nirlan's encouragement, though. A faint scent of amusement and bloodlust floated off the demon's skin. He was enjoying this. He was already sure of his imminent victory.

Azreth glanced over his shoulder to look for Raiya. She and the others were wisely standing back. He was glad they knew better than to try to help.

Raiya looked up at a balcony on the second floor. Careful to keep the other demon in his peripheral vision, Azreth followed her gaze. A human was perched there in the shadows, watching them. Azreth recognized him immediately, even hidden in the shadows, as if the man's blackened soul called out to him.

"Nirlan!" Raiya's voice snapped like a whip, and Nirlan reacted as if he'd been struck. He turned and ran out of sight.

"*Go!*" Azreth shouted to Raiya, and she jumped at the volume of his voice. "Go after him!"

Claws sliced across his chest. He recoiled, blindly throwing out a wave of amorphous magic. It knocked the other demon back, but it was all wild strength and no finesse. Touching a hand to his chest, Azreth felt blood where the claws had cut deep. He let it bleed. He couldn't afford to expend magic on healing superficial wounds—he might need every last drop to fight.

The other demon watched Raiya and the others run up the stairs, following her movement with the bright, sharp eyes of a hunter. Interest showed in his expression, and for a horrible moment, Azreth thought he was going to chase her. But the demon turned to him instead, unhurried.

"Where do you come from?" Azreth blurted.

The demon paused, probably surprised to hear him speak at a

time like this. Demons didn't bother exchanging words when there was blood to be shed. Azreth didn't know why he'd asked the question. It was the sort of immaterial, pointless thing that mortals asked strangers to be polite. But it was what came to mind as he searched for anything that would delay another attack.

The demon started to move, and Azreth quickly spoke again. "I can help you destroy the mortal who bound you."

The demon paused again. "You wish to serve me?"

Azreth's entire being rebelled at the idea of being put into servitude again.

"A wise offer," the demon said.

"I am no servant," Azreth said sharply. "We can work together to kill the mortal and then go our separate ways, as equals."

The demon stared at him, bemused.

It was a ridiculous thing to say. It was what Raiya would have suggested. A very short time ago, he had reacted with that same bemusement when she'd made this offer to him. This simply was not the way of the kin.

"Serve me, or die. I will let you choose," the demon said.

Azreth was afraid. And the other demon could certainly sense it, because Azreth was having a shocking amount of difficulty suppressing his feelings. Perhaps spending so much time among mortals, who felt their emotions so freely, had given him bad habits.

Or maybe it was just that he'd never had so much to lose.

"I am no servant," he repeated.

The demon looked amused. "Perhaps you will change your mind." And then he lunged.

Azreth twisted sideways, then backed up another step, and then another, as attacks kept coming. A long talon grazed him, ripping open his forearm. He hissed, lashing out with a spear of magic. It missed, but as the demon came at him again,

Azreth dove under his arm and swiped at his thigh with a summoned blade. A cut opened above the demon's knee, but it did little to slow him down.

They traded blows for what felt like hours but must have been only minutes. Soon they were both adorned with bruises and cuts, and the stones of the walls and floor around them were cracked from the impacts of their bodies.

As Azreth tired, he grew more desperate. He feinted with a longsword and then summoned a smaller dagger to stab at the demon's opposite side when he leaned away from the feint. He put all his weight behind the attack to ensure it hit home, driving the dagger in just below his ribs.

The demon grunted in pain, but Azreth felt no sense of victory from landing the blow, because he knew he'd overextended, leaving himself open to a counterattack.

The demon grabbed him by the shoulders and slammed him into the wall. The back of Azreth's head hit stone. His vision spotted with black, and then he was on the ground in a pile of rubble, his head throbbing.

The demon stood over him, breathing hard as he flicked blood from his claws—but Azreth's attention was drawn to something behind him.

Paladin Adamus stood behind the demon, bow and iron-tipped arrow clenched tightly in both hands, his face ghostly white. Azreth couldn't imagine why he hadn't left with the others, and for a moment he wondered if he'd been waiting for an opportunity to stab Azreth in the back. But as the demon stepped toward Azreth, Adamus drew the bow and shot at the demon's back.

The demon shouted, a sound that shook the flagstones beneath them. Blood sizzled as it burned on the iron. He spun, reaching behind himself to rip the shaft from his back. The arrow clattered to the ground. The Paladin should have run with the others, the fool. But instead, he'd given Azreth an opening.

Azreth summoned another sword of magenta light, which he gripped in his flesh-and-blood hand because he didn't know how much longer he could maintain his summoned arm. Adamus turned to run, but the demon reached out to him with a tendril of magic, lifting the Paladin off his feet. As the demon threw him to the ground, knocking him unconscious—or maybe killing him—Azreth dragged himself up from the floor and lunged.

The demon spun to face him, too late. The blade sank into his chest.

His claws lashed out, cutting everything in reach—Azreth's arm, his side, his chest. Azreth didn't try to evade them. He let the attacks come as he pushed the sword harder, cutting deeper. There was a crunch as the blade hit bone. Black gore spilled from the demon's body. For a moment, he thought he might actually win this fight. If his blade had been iron instead of mere magic, maybe he would have. But bright particles of healing magic were already covering the demon's wounds.

And then something hit Azreth just above his navel.

It took his breath. All his muscles froze in place. His summoned arm and his sword faded away as he lost concentration on his spells. He looked down, and the demon's hand was buried in his abdomen. The claws had cut through him like a knife.

The demon dragged his claws up Azreth's body, ripping through organs and skin. When he'd torn a jagged gash from his waist to his sternum, he threw him to the ground.

Even knowing this injury was too grievous to recover from, Azreth tried to get up. He gave up when the demon's boot came down hard on his chest, pushing the wind from his lungs. He gritted his teeth. Something in his chest bubbled, and hot blood oozed over his skin. He put his hand to his stomach, and a frail healing spell began to form, but then it guttered out. His magic was spent.

He glanced over at Paladin Adamus, who was not moving. There would be no more help from him. Azreth also could no longer sense Raiya nearby. He hoped she had gotten far away.

The demon stood over him, grimacing as the hole in his own chest rapidly closed. He spat blood on the ground. "Why bother fighting?" he asked. "What do you have to gain from prolonging a fight you can't win? Are you really so foolish?"

His disgust was both so familiar and so foreign.

For all of his life, Azreth had thought it was only natural to be disgusted by weakness. He had perfectly understood why his maker had hated him, because when he saw a creature that was deformed or injured or small, or when he witnessed a display of unguarded emotion, he'd felt the same deep discomfort she had felt.

He had seen himself in those small, vulnerable creatures. He hated himself, so he hated them, too.

The demon leaned closer, as if searching for the flaw that would explain Azreth's behavior. His nose wrinkled, and he said accusingly, "I know this scent. You smell like desperation and misguided happiness. You're ill."

"Perhaps," Azreth said. The demon couldn't have understood, and Azreth pitied him. He couldn't know what it was like to be enthralled. He would never know this joy.

"Can you not see how broken you are?" the demon asked. "Have you no regret?"

"I have no regret for serving the one I love." Something in his lungs sputtered when he spoke and breathed. He shuddered slightly as he fought to stay conscious.

"If I were kinder, I would put you out of your misery," the demon said. He waved a short spell over Azreth, healing him —but only barely. Azreth gingerly touched his chest, taking a gurgling breath. The wound was still bleeding, but he did not think it would kill him yet. "Perhaps I should bring you back to the hells to be exorcised."

Azreth knew it was a false threat designed to frighten him, but a thread of panic still went through him. The demon smirked, taunting him, but he had no idea what the threat truly meant.

Azreth's mind was the one thing that had always been his own. The idea of the core of his being—his feelings, his love for Raiya and the mortal world—being stripped from him, was horrific. He understood now why the enthralled fought their exorcisms so desperately.

The demon bent to pick up Paladin Adamus in one arm, then took Azreth's wrist to drag him behind him. "Don't die just yet," he said. Azreth could feel him feeding from his agony as they moved down the hall.

TWENTY-FIVE

Azreth swung in and out of consciousness as the demon dragged him through the castle.

After a while, he realized he was no longer moving. Unpleasant sensations told him he was still alive: blunt pain in his abdomen, cold stone on his back, and light pressing against his closed eyes. He forced his eyes open, squinting against the obscene amount of magic in the room. It flowed in glittering rivers through the air, along the walls, through luminescent runes and onward. It originated from a point somewhere beyond his line of sight.

He tilted his head to look around the room. He was in a familiar place. It was the very room where he'd first been summoned. The place of his imprisonment.

The crimson-skinned demon, seated in a chair near him, was looking down at him with a bored expression, as if to convey that Azreth had been too weak an opponent to excite him. He'd healed himself, and probably only the iron-poisoned wound in his back remained.

Azreth saw movement out of the corner of his eye, and he looked up. Nirlan was standing nearby with his back to them, fiddling with something on a table. There was nothing standing between them except the fact that Azreth didn't have the strength to move.

Beyond Nirlan was the point from which all the magic in the room was flowing: a huge, shining tear in space between this plane and another.

It was a gate to the hells. That was how Nirlan had brought so many creatures here. Azreth wondered whether he'd intentionally brought them here, or if that had just been a side effect of his carelessness in summoning the second demon.

"Azreth," came a small voice.

He forced his head back to look behind him, though it made the wound in his chest stretch excruciatingly. Behind him on the floor, shakily holding herself up on her elbows, was Raiya.

She was still here.

She hadn't run.

She was here, in danger, and he couldn't protect her.

Azreth looked up at the other demon, who was already looking back at him as if he'd read his thoughts. Azreth's jaw stiffened as he tried to stifle his emotions, but there was no point. The demon already knew his secret: Azreth was enthralled by Raiya. If Nirlan allowed it, he would hurt Raiya just to hurt Azreth. His pain would probably taste exquisite.

Nirlan turned to Raiya, clasping his ugly, rodent-like hands together. His voice was just as insufferably arrogant as Azreth remembered. "I can't lie—it stings that the first thing out of your mouth when you awaken is another man's name."

Raiya bared her teeth. Under the strange light of the gate, they were the same ghostly greenish shade as her skin. She didn't look injured yet, only weakened, as if by a spell or drug. Nirlan had done something to her. "You said he wasn't bound to you," she said, jerking her head toward the crimson-skinned demon.

"And you believed me," Nirlan said flatly.

Heavy, ugly emotion flowed from Raiya, savory and yet utterly unpalatable.

"You're not so mouthy without your weapon," Nirlan said to her.

"You opened a gate to the hells. Why?"

"That part was incidental. The priestess looked at Eunaios's work from the last summoning, but she didn't fully understand it. She said this was the best way for her to adapt his spellwork to connect to the hells and find another demon to bind."

"This is madness. Anything could come through it."

"I can find a way to close it later. The important thing was finding the demon."

"But why? Why is it so important to you?"

Sudden anger billowed from Nirlan. "Because you *disrespected* me, you unfaithful—!" He cut himself off. For a moment, Azreth thought he was going to strike her. But Nirlan lowered his voice, starting over. "Because you deserve this. You were a fool if you thought you could cheat me out of my wife and my demon."

Something nearby shifted. Azreth and Raiya both looked up to see Jai on the floor nearby, moving a little, but not quite awake. Beside her was Madira, unconscious, and Adamus. Not one of them had escaped.

"Let them go," Raiya said to Nirlan. "Please."

"Why?"

"They're just children."

"If they're old enough to fight, they're old enough to die."

Anger and despair pulled at her lips. "Bastard."

"Ah, there's that mouth." Nirlan crossed the floor unhurriedly, then bent to take Raiya's chin in his hand. She grimaced, stiff in his grasp, but she didn't have the strength to fight him. Dread and anger and humiliation flowed from her, and as much Azreth disliked it, it made his body cramp with hunger.

He glanced up at the demon, who lounged comfortably in his chair despite the fact that it was several sizes too small for him. Bright red eyes slanted down to meet his, alert but disinterested. He had certainly guessed what Azreth was thinking: if Azreth could feed from her, he might be able to regain a scrap of strength. He might be able to help her. The demon just tilted his mouth into a smirk.

"Don't condescend to me," Raiya said to Nirlan, and the demon's attention shifted back to them.

"You think you don't deserve it?" Nirlan replied.

Nearby, Madira shifted slowly, raising a hand to his head. Wincing, he opened his eyes, and his gaze eventually landed on Azreth. Jai and Adamus were still motionless.

Azreth's eyes went to Adamus's hip. His bow was gone, but his iron sword was still tucked in its scabbard at his side.

Nirlan bent over Raiya, holding her as she tried to pull away. "You'll come crawling back to me now," he said quietly, confidently. "Kiss me. Be a good girl."

Azreth realized that he'd never known what true hatred of a person felt like, the way mortals felt it, until that moment. Anything he'd felt before must have been mere dislike.

Raiya's mouth was a straight, hard line as she met her husband's eyes. "Fine," she said.

Something in her voice had changed.

She was going to kill him. Azreth didn't know how, but she was going to save them all, just like she'd saved them from the vythian.

Nirlan didn't notice. He was too stupid and arrogant to see what was plain. Despite sleeping at Raiya's side every night for months while they were husband and wife, he didn't know her.

He looked at Azreth, gloating. "No man will take what's mine. And no demon, for that matter. Not without suffering dearly."

Raiya's hand began to move. Azreth watched as she surreptitiously reached toward a pile of clutter beside her. Her bag had been dumped out, its contents scattered. Though she never broke eye contact with Nirlan, she was reaching for a glinting, silver object with a sharp, pointed end. Her enchanting stylus. Azreth stopped breathing.

"You're worthless without me," Nirlan whispered to her. "Never forget that. Never forget this moment."

"I won't," Raiya said. Then, without a trace of mercy, she stabbed the stylus into his throat.

Blood gushed from Nirlan's neck. It had pierced an artery. She'd struck perfectly, beautifully. Like she'd been born to kill him. Like it was fated. Blood and hunger roared in Azreth's ears. Raiya's triumph filled him, and he felt lighter, stronger. Mesmerized, he watched her raise her arm high and stab again and again, until Nirlan was on the floor beneath her and she was drenched with his blood. He wished the moment would last forever. He'd never loved her more.

He looked down at his palm. The runes on his skin had gone dark. The marks remained for now, but the enchantment had perished along with his binder.

As Raiya stopped, breathing hard over Nirlan's body, the demon in the chair moved. Azreth braced himself, but the demon was moving past him, toward Raiya.

Azreth rolled over and sat up. He heard a wet sound—his own blood hitting the floor. His torn abdominal muscles screamed in protest as he struggled to his knees. Pain and blood loss made his head pound.

"Madira!" he shouted. "The Paladin's sword—"

The boy was still not fully awake. He must have been sedated by the same thing Raiya had been. He gave Azreth a confused look, his eyes distant.

Azreth crawled to Adamus's sword, but the iron repelled him almost magnetically. His fingers were trembling before he'd even touched the hilt. The miasma of iron was too toxic.

"Here," came a slurred voice.

Azreth turned to find Madira offering him a bundle of black cloth. His cloak. Azreth grabbed it, wrapped it around his hand, and grasped the hilt of the sword with it.

Ice and fire shot up his arm. The iron was a choking poison, an arc of lightning a hair's breadth from his flesh. His grip weakened, and the sword almost fell from his hand. Steeling himself, he tightened his grip and yanked the sword from its scabbard. It nearly made him faint.

He took a step toward Raiya, and then another. His body was numb, and his feet and hand were somehow not his own, as if he were controlling his body from afar.

The demon stood between Raiya and himself. Looming over her, trapping her against the wall, he reached toward her with a clawed hand. Azreth staggered toward them, but he was slow. The demon began to cut into her.

He felt Raiya's fear rising and then peaking into panic. Her pain burst forth like fiery, glaring sunlight.

Azreth didn't resist. He followed the alluring, sickening scent of it. He let it feed him. It tasted wonderful and terrible as he drank it down. It gave him strength.

Raising the sword, he surged forward.

There was a damp crunch.

His hazy vision focused. Red and black swam in front of him—black liquid foaming and steaming as it flowed over crimson skin. The sword was deep in the demon's back.

Azreth released the hilt, leaving it buried. He couldn't feel his hand, but that seemed of little consequence now. Raiya staggered away from the demon, holding her hand over her stomach. She was alive.

As she ran for the table, Azreth's knees gave out. He dropped to the floor, his ears ringing, as he watched Raiya pick up her bow from the table and point an arrow toward the demon.

"Get back!" she shouted, cornering him against the shimmering gate.

The demon was doubled over in pain. He gave her a dark look, and Azreth feared he would somehow keep fighting despite the iron weakening him.

Raiya drew the bowstring taut. "Go!" she snarled, her arms shaking.

There was a tense pause. And then the demon backed away. The surface of the portal rippled as he retreated into it, as if he'd sunk beneath the surface of a pond.

It was over.

Raiya lowered her bow, her shoulders slumping. Then she turned to him.

"Azreth," she breathed, hurrying to his side. He reached out to her, and a hundred cuts and burns and bruises all over his body lit up with pain, but he could hardly feel them as she embraced him.

Twenty-Six

In a dark, windowless room, Azreth lay curled inside a fireplace, flames caressing his skin. The stinging warmth was a balm on both his physical wounds and his soul alike. The smoke reminded him of the fourth hell, and for some reason, despite how much he never wanted to go back, it was comforting.

After they'd killed Nirlan and banished the demon, Azreth had retreated to one of the castle's smaller bedrooms. Raiya and the others had set to work building a barricade of iron implements around the gate to discourage anything else from coming through. They would guard the gate while he healed. They were safe, for now. It was over.

Wasn't it?

Then what was this lingering uncertainty he felt? Why was there still a scrap of fear fluttering inside him, even when he had so much to be glad for?

Behind him, the door clicked open. There was a surprised intake of breath. He turned over to find Raiya in the doorway.

"Azreth. Are you all right?" she asked.

He slowly sat up, holding his hand out just beyond the flames. He didn't want to leave their warmth just yet.

Coming to kneel on the flagstones, she touched his fingertips cautiously, as though his fresh-from-the-fire skin might burn her—a possibility which had not occurred to him, but should have. When she decided it was safe, she closed her hand around his last three fingers, lifting her eyes to meet his.

"What do you need?" she asked.

A soft, pleasant emotion stirred in his chest. The enthrallment. It had become a comfort instead of something that frightened and shamed him.

"Nothing," he said automatically. At first, he'd thought he had nothing more to say. But Raiya's silence opened space for him to think, and then to think aloud.

"I have feelings I don't know how to name," he said slowly. "I have experienced many unfamiliar feelings since I came to your plane, and since I began to love you."

A small, pleased smile curved her lips when he said the word "love." The way she smiled at him felt like a ray of light, as warm as the flames.

He was not in the habit of thinking about these things in such explicit terms, let alone saying them aloud. But Raiya liked hearing him speak, and he realized he liked telling her his thoughts. He could tell her anything, even things that seemed too frivolous to bother someone with.

"I think, maybe, I have had these feelings for longer than that. I think I did not want to see them. Demons pretend they feel nothing but hunger and anger and lust, because that's all we need to survive. Anything else only makes life more difficult."

Raiya gave him a look. "That's what I've been telling you for ages, you silly ox." He felt slightly foolish, because it was true. She squeezed his fingers, prodding him further. "How do you feel right now?"

How did he feel? After all this?

He felt like he was baring his throat to the world and daring it to strike him down.

He climbed out of the fire, flames sparking and sputtering around him. Tendrils of smoke rose from his body, and ashes coated his skin. He looked down at himself, studying the new scars the other demon had given him. They were bad memories written into him, taking their place among dozens of other bad memories.

Raiya was still holding his hand.

"I feel happy," he said. "But I am also afraid. Because I don't know what comes next."

"That's for us to decide, isn't it?"

"I don't know how to be a demon living peacefully in the mortal plane. It is not done."

"It is now. You can be the first."

"The first?" He lifted an eyebrow. "Do you think there will be more?"

"I doubt you'll be the only one. I doubt you're even the first, in fact."

He wished he was as certain as she was. Perhaps he'd seen too much of demonkind to see the potential for goodness in them anymore.

"Raiya, I have never loved someone before. Love is a mortal thing."

"So you keep telling me."

"Yes. And because of this, I must do something else I'm unaccustomed to. I must ask for your help. You have helped me learn how to be equals. I want you to teach me how to love, also. You speak about love as if it's always a good thing, but I know it's possible to love badly and to hurt yourself or others with this madness."

She seemed pleased. "I will help you love well, as long as you do the same for me."

It had not occurred to him that she might return his request. He couldn't think of a way for her to be better to him. She was already perfect. He almost said so, but he could predict what she'd say in response: *No one is perfect. And even demons have needs. You're no different from mortals.*

"Raiya. In the dungeon, I fed from you," he confessed. He spoke so quietly it was almost a whisper. "He was killing you, and I used your pain. I strengthened myself with it. I... liked it. I don't know if I can rightfully claim to love you when I have enjoyed your pain."

This time, she didn't have a quick answer ready. She frowned a little, surprised.

"I do not like what I am," he said. "I don't want to be a monster. But I am afraid I can't be anything else." He tried to pull his hand away from hers, but she tightened her grip on his fingers.

"I never asked you to be anything else. If you were anything else, we wouldn't be here right now."

"I am still sorry."

"Be at ease, Azreth."

He frowned at her, fearing she wasn't taking him seriously. This was serious.

"You did not hurt me," she said. "You did not betray me. You protected me. And don't you dare say that you don't love me. You did something you abhorred, something that caused you pain, in order to protect me. Is that not love?"

"That's an ugly sort of love."

"Perhaps. Life isn't always clean and perfect, is it? Sometimes good things are intertwined with the bad, and we have to sort things out as best we can." She leaned closer, making sure he was looking her in the eye and taking in every word she said. "I don't want your shame. It does neither of us any good. I want your strength, your empathy, your humility, your curiosity, and all the other lovely things that make you wonderful. I don't want anything else. I will never ask you to be something you cannot be."

Her steadfast belief in him made him want to become better. Maybe she was right about him. Maybe he really could be a force of good in this world, like she was. Maybe, someday, people would look upon him not with fear and hatred, but with friendship and gratitude.

He bit his tongue for a long time, then said, "Tell me a service I can perform to earn your forgiveness."

Raiya grew exasperated. "I require no service."

"Please."

She sighed, looking away, but he could see her thinking it over. Eventually she turned to him again, smiling. "Fine. I'll give you a task to perform for me, but only if you give me one in exchange."

He supposed that was the best he was going to get. "If that's what you need."

She nodded, satisfied. "Kiss me."

"That is not a service."

"Why? Because you enjoy it?"

"Yes."

"I don't see why that has any bearing on it."

He couldn't argue with that.

He bent over her and gave her the best, softest kiss he could manage. He didn't know how mortals measured the quality of a kiss, but he knew that when Raiya kissed him like this, he felt like fire was coursing through him, and he hoped she felt the same way.

She smiled triumphantly when he pulled away. "All right. Tell me something I can do for you."

He hesitated, afraid to say what was on the tip of his tongue. But someone who loved well would be truthful. Someone who loved well would lay themselves bare without fear of judgment or pain.

"I like your voice," he said. And then, quietly, because this felt so shameful to admit, "I like hearing you say kind things to me."

Raiya just stroked his hair, and he found that the absence of her voice did nothing to detract from his love for her, either.

"You are good enough," she said after a while. Her hand shifted to his cheek as she studied him. "I love how clever you are, and how thoughtful and kind. I love your resilience and strength. When I'm with you, I feel braver, steadier. And gods, your beauty makes my knees weak..."

He interrupted her to press his lips against hers again. He wrapped his arm around her waist, pulling her against him, and she made a soft, surprised sound against his mouth as she arched her back. Her hands splayed on his chest, and her fingers flexed against him as heated desire began to scent her skin.

But then her hands wandered too close to the healing wound beneath his ribs, and his breath caught. She quickly let go of him.

"Sorry. I forgot," she said.

"You didn't hurt me."

She touched his chest lightly. "You deserve all the pleasure in the world. And I intend to help you find it... Right after you're in one piece again."

He leaned in, lowering his voice as he brushed his lips against her. "There is no need to wait. You can be gentle, can't you?"

He felt her grin against his skin. "Always."

Demon Bound is an adventurous, angsty, sweet & spicy standalone set in the high fantasy Ardani universe. This book tells the story of Hell Sent from Raiya's perspective.

Free Bonus Epilogue

Newsletter subscribers can download a free short story/epilogue about Raiya and Azreth, *Sanctuary*. This content isn't available anywhere else, so sign up for the newsletter via my website to read it!

Thank You

Thank you for reading Hell Sent! If you enjoyed this book, please consider supporting my work by leaving a rating or review. It doesn't have to be long—just a few words is fine—and it really does help!

If you're new to my books, I hope you loved this introduction to the Ardani universe. If you're eager for more, try Elves of Ardani: a series of fantasy romance standalones with plenty more spice, angst, and adventure for you to binge on.

As always, I owe a big thank-you to all my readers. Your support means so much. I feel privileged to be able to share my world and characters with you all, and knowing that other people are enjoying my books along with me is a big part of what keeps me writing.

Special thanks to my many beta readers for this book (Shanon, Kylie, Dana, Kristyn, Andrea, Alice, Dani, Amber, Danielle, Sara, Kate, and Tania) for all your much-needed help. Extra special thanks to my parents for accepting and nurturing my obsession with fiction, and to my wonderful partner for being endlessly supportive of me and my writing career.

— Nina

About the Author

Nina K. Westra is an elf enthusiast and fantasy romance author with a love of antiheroes, outsiders, and feminist men. Her books feature sweetness and spice, action and adventure, and heart-wrenching (usually forbidden, always angsty) romance with non-human men.

She lives in the ridiculously beautiful Pacific Northwest, and when she's not writing, she can usually be found petting someone's cat.

For news, ARCs, and free stories, sign up for her newsletter at ninakwestra.com

instagram.com/ninakwestra
facebook.com/NinaKWestra
bookbub.com/profile/nina-k-westra

www.ingramcontent.com/pod-product-compliance
Lightning Source LLC
Chambersburg PA
CBHW011853300726
48970CB00009B/2777